I0549127

Keeper of the Key

Volume 3 of the 'Keeper House' series

A Novel by W. E. NOEL

DEDICATION

With love and gratitude to my wife, children and
Family who have always shown me I could be more
than I thought I could be.

Copyright © 2016 NOEL & COMPANY

All rights reserved.

ISBN: 978-0-9981961-1-4

FOREWARD

This novel, number three in the series, is based on the fictitious
murder of the Keeper Family early in the 20thcentury. All of the
characters, names and events in this book are fictitious, and any
resemblance to actual persons, living or dead, is purely
coincidental.

CHAPTER 1

"Grab that damn paddle and shock him!" Dr. Greybar yelled. "He's going to die if you don't move! Now MOVE! Damn it." Dr. Greybar did not know how much longer he could hold onto the bleeding artery of the man on the floor of his office. He needed Amanda, his head nurse, to hurry and bring clamps and sutures so he could get this man's bleeding stopped and help the others save the fellow with two bullets in him. "Increase it to 300 and hit him again," Dr. Greybar told the nurse. He did not like the way the other man's body was NOT responding to the electro-shock to stimulate his heart. He knew that every second that they did not get it restarted, took minutes off his life. He watched as the nurses turned the dials on the machine and yelled "clear." Again, he laid on the marble floor in a pool of his blood and remained lifeless. His heart had not beat on its' own for several minutes now, and the doctor had to make another decision. "Do I let this fellow bleed out to save the other man, or do I watch and hope that an RNA nurse can get his heart started?" That is the question going through Dr. Greybar's head right at this moment.

Suddenly Amanda appeared with a container full of sterilized clamps and suturing equipment. The doctor told her what had to be done as he continued to clamp both hands around the artery of the bleeding man and watch the nurses attempt to get the other man's heart resuscitated. Dr. Greybar moved his hands slightly as Amanda reached into the man's abdomen to carefully place clamps on vital arterial locations and check the outflow of his blood.

"Damn it, nurse, don't wait for him to ask you out on a date, get the damn paddles on him again; he's running out of time!" Dr. Greybar yelled again. It could not be any more frustrating of a morning for the staff. All of them, with the exception of Amanda had not had this kind of incident happen to them, not even in nursing school. This was something that they attempted to simulate in training, but simulations never come anywhere close to reality. Now, the nurses knew that, too.

Suddenly, a young man of thirty-ish came running across the floor, throwing his suit coat onto chairs there in the waiting room, and grabbing the paddles away from the young, very nervous, nurse.

"Everyone clear away and turn it up one more notch." The young man yelled. "Clear!" he yelled as he applied the paddles to the man's chest, sending a shock throughout his body. His arms and hands seem to bounce off the marble floor as his feet kicked upward an inch or two before laying still again. The young man then checked for a heartbeat. He reached across the man's body and took the stethoscope off the young nurse and listened more intently before saying "he has a beat. It's not a good rhythm yet, but it's a heartbeat. Let's carefully get him up off the floor onto a gurney and get some blood into him before we lose him to something else."

Dr. Greybar watched what was happening while also watching Amanda apply the clamps in very strategic locations in order to prevent this man from bleeding out. "Young man, you had better be a licensed physician or you just opened yourself up to a possible lawsuit." Dr. Greybar said as he watched the man assist the nurses in lifting the man onto a gurney and elevate him. "And, I'm guessing that you're a doctor." The doctor started to release his grip on the other man's artery and watched as Amanda handed him a needle ready for his use. "By the way, very nice job! You may have saved his life."

"Thank you, Dr. Greybar, but he is not out of the woods, yet. We still have work to do." He said. "By the way, are all your Monday mornings this busy, or is this simply for my benefit?"

"Probably more for your benefit; this is not a typical Monday. Most Mondays are much busier," Dr. Greybar said. "I assume that you are Dr. Walker, my new partner?"

"Yes I am," the young man answered. "I would shake hands with you but we both have our hands inside bodies while trying to save these men's lives." The young man continued to try to stabilize the wounded man's heartbeat and blood pressure readings. As he continued to work, the nurses seemed to gather around and ask what they could do to assist. He asked one of them to prepare a hypodermic of epinephrine for injection into the man's heart to help stabilize his heartbeat. One of the young nurses got the key to the medicine vault from Amanda and went to get the hypodermic readied.

"Well," said Dr. Greybar, "I've got my guy stabilized and ready to transport to the hospital. How you doin' there, Walker? We still need to fish two slugs out of that man's body when you're ready. I do not feel we can leave that task for the ER docs, as they might receive a corpse if we wait that long."

"I agree, Dr. Greybar. I'm getting a good solid beat now and his BP is higher. Let's give him five minutes and then we can put him under." Said Dr. Walker.

When both doctors had finished removing two bullets from the man's upper torso, Dr. Greybar had Amanda phone the police to report that the two men were sedated, secured to their gurneys with plastic ties, and ready for the police department to pick up and take to the jail ward of the hospital. He knew that the police would have plenty of questions to ask, but he was not in a mood to be playing silly games with young cops whose only task in this office was to complete some department forms with verbiage. He has patients to see and sick people to heal, and just lacks any patience for trivial tasks that do not create any more time for him or his patients.

He scrubbed his hands and splashed cool water on his

face before turning to speak to Dr. Walker. "Care for some single malt, Dr. Walker?" he asked as he walked to a glass-fronted bookcase. Dr. Greybar opened the right door and watched as the entire false front of medical books dropped down out of sight. Left glimmering in the cabinet light was a prize collection of some of the world's finest, and some of the oldest, scotch whiskeys to be found. He reached in and removed two glasses and put them on his desk. "Dr. Walker?" he asked again.

Dr. Gerald Walker was not unaccustomed to fine scotch; his father, Montgomery Walker, was accustomed to having an occasional sip of 30 or 50 year old single malt and had allowed his sons to join him after they became legal drinking age. He wondered, though, if they had to see patients this afternoon, if having a drink was a prudent idea.

However, he knew that it would be a good way to cement the beginning of a medical-business relationship and decided to keep his intake to the very minimum. "Yes, thank you Dr. Greybar, I would like to join you in a little single malt. It may help to get the rest of the day put into order."

As Dr. Greybar poured two fingers of scotch into each glass, Dr. Walker looked around the office. It was very clean, but not very modern. Old style desk, old style possibly Victorian-age table and six chairs, and two very old combination bookshelf and drawer units, one of which had been modified to hide the doctor's fine collection of scotch. Dr. Greybar's office was very much the opposite of the clinic's entry, waiting room and exam rooms. It was as if Dr. Greybar had chosen to stay in an era from long ago.

"Here's to less busy days, and more busy days, doctor," Dr. Graybar said as he clinked his glass with the glass held by Dr. Walker.

Dr. Walker tipped his glass toward Dr. Greybar and said, "here's to good health and a long future for us both." Dr. Greybar smiled and drank his two fingers of scotch down with one gulp. Dr. Walker took a short sip and swallow of his scotch and marveled at how tasty and smooth it was. Scotch this good, he thought, could be very dangerous; especially on stressful days.

As the two doctors sat down at the table to talk for a moment, yelling and screaming came through from the outer offices, and Amanda knocked on office door before sticking her head in.

"Doctors, we have a bit of a situation our here with one of the patients," Amanda said. "The one man is nearly loose from one of his restraints and is threatening the nurses."

With that, the doctors jumped up from their chairs and ran out of the office into the hallway where the man who they had removed two bullets from, was wrestling with a loosened plastic tie and attempting to get his one arm free. Without hesitating, Dr. Walker walked up to the man and put a very firm grip around the man's throat causing him to go limp and struggle for air.

"Nurse, sedate this man right away, before he succumbs from lack of oxygen." Dr. Walker said, as he tightened his grip on the man's throat completely cutting off his breathing.

Almost as the doctor was finishing his instruction, Amanda approached holding a hypodermic and sent the man into his own dreamland. It took several minutes before the atmosphere in the waiting room, and the adjacent hallway, calmed down and returned to normal. The doctors decided to return to their talking, and to their single malt.

After nearly ten minutes of discussing the clinic and various nurses and patients, their discussion was interrupted by another knock on the door, and Amanda, once again, sticking her head through the doorway.

"Doctor, Mrs. Fitzpatrick is here for her follow-up appointment and you know how she is about waiting long. Shall I show her to exam room 4?" Amanda asked. "Yes. Yes. Show her to exam 4 and doctor Walker and I will be right there." Answered Dr. Greybar. It wasn't easy for Dr. Greybar to NOT get another two fingers. Instead, he set his glass in his office sink and started off to exam room 4. He asked Dr. Walker to accompany him and meet the charming Mrs. Fitzpatrick, whose entire family were all patients of the clinic. The Fitzpatrick family had been coming to this clinic since Gerald and Maureen Fitzpatrick were born; and they always paid their bill right away, with cash. The Fitzpatrick's were old, New England Irish people who came to the U.S. to escape the Irish Potato Famine. They started businesses in hostelry, metals, auto manufacturing, and eventually into the oil & gas industries. They made their millions in every endeavor and often were competing with the Kennedy family of Massachusetts. The Fitzpatrick's stayed in Connecticut, and let the Kennedy's have Massachusetts. Later generations of the Fitzpatrick clan got into state and national politics, with a son, Daniel Fitzpatrick, currently serving as the state's lieutenant governor.

Mrs. Fitzpatrick raised an eyebrow when Dr. Greybar introduced the new Dr. Walker to her as his new business partner, and co-owner of the clinic. Mrs. Fitzpatrick was not too certain she liked anything 'new', or anyone quite as young as Dr. Walker is.

"Walker? Walker?" she asked. "I know the Walkers of Huntington, New York. Any relation?"

"Yes, Mrs. Fitzpatrick, they are my parents." Dr. Walker said.

"Oh, I see," was Mrs. Fitzpatrick's response. She carefully inspected the younger Dr. Walker with a slow moving look, and one eyebrow raised.

He could tell from her body language that he was not a 'welcomed' visitor with Dr. Greybar. "Would you prefer that I leave Mrs. Fitzpatrick?" he asked her, expecting a fast "yes" reply. She looked at Dr. Walker standing there with a pink stethoscope around his neck, she then looked at Dr. Greybar with a smirk on his face, and said "no, you can stay. I don't have anything that you haven't seen already...only older! Much older."

Dr. Walker chuckled a little and asked Amanda for Mrs. Fitzpatrick's file.

The rest of Mrs. Fitzpatrick's visit went very smoothly and without much conversation. She had come in for her follow-up exam from an operation done last year, and, just as Dr. Greybar said, paid for everything when she left including a prescription she picked up while in the office.

As she started to open the office door, she turned and told Dr. Walker, "tell your parents that Maureen Fitzpatrick sends them my regards and hopes to see them at the Yale Regatta this year."

With that, she went through the office door and into her waiting limousine.

It was perfect timing for Mrs. Fitzpatrick's exit as the New Haven police department arrived with an entourage of uniformed personnel to handle the two men that the doctors had worked on to save their lives.

A police sergeant with a name badge of "Kelly" came in with a clipboard and pen in hand, ready to take down all information from the doctors.

Sergeant Kelly began asking his barrage of questions, most of which Dr. Walker could not answer because much of what happened, happened prior to his arriving at the clinic. The police asked questions of every staff member for another fifteen minutes before putting handcuffs on both men and transferring them to police department ambulance gurneys for transporting to the hospital.

When Sergeant Kelly was satisfied that they had taken down all the information, gotten all the facts of what had occurred, and sipped a little of Dr. Greybar's single malt, the entire group of police officers departed.

Apparently, whether you are an on-duty policeman, or an on-duty doctor, a 'finger or two' of Dr. Greybar's Glenmorangie 25 year old single malt scotch is simply paying your respects to both the doctor and the distillery.

The balance of the day was pretty routine, with patients every fifteen minutes until four o'clock. Then it was as if someone locked the front door and no one tried to open it. All the streams of people, old men, young women, young men, older women, and children simply stopped.

Dr. Greybar told Dr. Walker that they kept pretty strict

14

office hours, and he used both Tuesday and Thursday mornings to make his rounds at the hospitals. He had enough time for each patient and time for his notes to be written down in each file. Dr. Walker did not say anything to the older Dr. Greybar, but he could foresee some updating of procedures, and equipment coming in the near future.

The doctor's office schedule seemed like a good, workable schedule to Dr. Walker, but he did not know if doing rounds only on Tuesday and Thursday mornings would continue, or not. Dr. Greybar is a very good doctor who is from a time long gone, and Dr. Walker likes many of the new technology tools that are available to assist doctors with their practices and their time. This is one of only a few areas where the younger, and the older, doctors differ in their thinking.

To Dr. Gerald Walker, it is somewhat amazing that he and Dr. Greybar ever got together in this clinic. It was the curmudgeon, old Dr. Greybar that had met the Walkers years ago, and became great friends, and sometimes golfing buddy, with Mr. Walker. As the years started to creep up on Dr. Greybar he sought out a younger, energetic, family-practice oriented doctor to take over his practice and allow him more time to work on his life's other loves: golf, gardening, reading and travel.

One day, while losing horribly in golf to Mr. Walker,

they began to talk about retirement, family and a whole myriad of other topics. When retirement plans came up, the conversation went on for a long time with Mr. Walker telling the doctor about his youngest son and his love of 'family practice' medicine in Rhode Island. The more they talked, over several more losing rounds of golf, the more compatible the two doctors began to sound. Mr. Walker, in the meantime, began to tell his son Gerald about the very beloved, and aging, Dr. Greybar and his desire to turn his practice over to someone younger.

After many, many phone calls, the two doctors worked out a deal for Dr. Walker to join the practice and began to take over the family clinic and buy Dr. Greybar out. Gerald Walker had his sister, Stephanie, draw up the contracts and agreements and, as the saying goes, "the rest is history." The buy out would take five years and would allow Dr. Greybar ample time to "ease into" a fuller retirement mode without the worries about income. And, Dr. Walker found that he and his family really like the New Haven area and being closer to his siblings and parents. Dr. Greybar called the entire arrangement a "win-win."

CHAPTER 2

As Sergeant Kelly was finishing the paperwork that had to accompany the two men being locked up in the jail ward at the Yale-New Haven Psychiatric Hospital, an on-duty young uniformed officer asked him if he knew the identity of both men they had secured in cells. The sergeant answered that they found a state issued identification card on one man, but the other was being booked as a 'John Doe.' The young officer said that it was difficult to say for certain, because of all the cuts and blood on John Doe's face and arms, but he resembled someone that the officer had seen a bulletin on back at the station. Sergeant Kelly said he would look through the bulletins when he got back to the station and see if he found someone resembling their John Doe. He then thanked the young officer for his keen eye and for speaking up.

Sergeant Kelly double checked the paperwork before giving a copy of the 'booking' documents to the floor nurse in charge. He then told one of the uniform officers on duty to be aware of the two men just brought in as one of them could be very dangerous as he tried to escape while under sedation at the doctor's office. With that, the sergeant folded his paperwork and left to go back to the police station to file everything; and, to check the recent bulletins.

The police station was a beehive of activity; not unusual for a weekday in a college town. There were officers doing paperwork on arrestees for shoplifting, arrestees for pick pocketing, and various other people waiting to be booked for breaking other laws of the land. Sergeant Kelly noticed, right away, that the average age of the arrestees was well above the normal, college age level, of the Friday –through-Sunday arrestees.

Sergeant Kelly found the stack of new bulletins that some rookie patrolman had not file away yet, and began to thumb through them one-by-one until he stopped on one that concerned him. It was an alert from the Connecticut State Police on behalf of the Federal Bureau of Investigation of an escape, and presumed dangerous, felon named George Kitchen. Seems this escapee, also was known as 'Guido Kiefer' and as 'Gerald Keeper', was being transported to the Allenwood, PA high-security men's prison when an auto accident, which involved their prison van, occurred and this George Kitchen escaped along with one other very dangerous felon. The bulletin said that it was believed that the two escaped felons had parted company and were traveling in different directions with George Kitchen believed headed for Canada.

As Sergeant Kelly studied the photo more, and more, it began to look a little like the badly bloodied, and wounded body of one of the arrestees they booked into the prison ward at the hospital. Perhaps the young patrol officer at the hospital was right; this was not a 'John Doe' after all, but is actually a 'George Kitchen', or 'Gerald Keeper.'

Sergeant Kelly studied the picture more closely before grabbing the phone and calling the jail ward at the hospital. When the officer on duty answered the phone, Sergeant Kelly identified himself and explained his reason for calling; he wanted two officers to check on the 'John Doe' fellow and secure his bindings more. Sergeant Kelly explained that he had a bulletin which showed a picture of an escapee from the 'Feds', and that the man pictured closely resembled Mr. 'John Doe.' He told the officer that he is finishing up at the station and coming back to the hospital with the picture. The officer acknowledged Sergeant Kelly's instructions and said that they would check 'John Doe' right away.

Sergeant Kelly finished his paperwork at the station, grabbed a copy of the bulletin and headed out to the hospital ward.

Yale-New Haven Psychiatric Hospital's activity level swings like a pendulum any hour of a day, and any day of a week. Some days it faintly resembles a cemetery, while other days it is non-stop pandemonium from sunrise to midnight. Today, it did not resemble a cemetery; it was fast-paced, never slowing, race of people pushing wheelchairs, people pushing gurneys, people trying to run from one ward to another, and people shouting out orders for one thing, or another. So it was not surprising that no one outside the jail ward heard the two gunshots when they occurred. The first shot at very close, point blank range into the young officers abdomen, and the second gunshot into the forehead of the second officer. Both officers lay on the floor of the ward room in pools of their own blood, while 'John Doe' cut the remaining restraints off his wrists and ankles. He wanted badly to put another round, or two, into each officer but thought he may have use for those rounds of ammo later. He yanked the IV out of his left arm, looked at the two dying officers and carefully made his way out of the room.

Sergeant Kelly was having difficulty making his way through the lobby with all the activity occurring on the first floor. He normally would stand aside as they wheeled someone past on a gurney, but now he was on a mission: to determine if one of the two detainees was, in fact, wanted by the FBI. He helped push the gurney down the hallway as far as the elevator he needed to go down to the jail wards. He pressed the down button and waited.

As he heard the creaking of the old elevator getting close, he was startled by a nurse shouting "Sergeant Kelly. Sergeant Kelly get down to the jail wards. Officers down." Sergeant Kelly watched the elevator door open and wondered if he had any faster way to go down one level. He pushed 'B' on the elevator panel and then pushed it again! He wished that the speed of the old elevator would increase in proportion to the force of his pushing 'B' on the panel, but it did not. Slowly, as if the door had a mind of it's own, the elevator door began to close and allow the elevator to begin its' downward descent to the jail wards. Ever so slowly it went; eventually arriving at the basement level as all the world waited for the elevator door to slowly open and allow the police sergeant to make a hasty exit to check on the well being of his officers.

The jail ward number 3 was vacant except for a uniform police office laying on the floor in a large pool of blood, and a uniform officer laying on the floor on the opposite side of the room with a single bullet hole in his forehead just slightly left of the center of his head. His eyes were wide open and enlarged as if in shock; there was very little blood pooling around his body.

No sooner had Sergeant Kelly surveyed jail ward 3 and saw that the arrestee 'John Doe' was not visible anywhere, than 2 doctors rushed into the room followed by several nurses and technicians. They quickly checked both officers vitals and confirmed that one police officer was dead from a single gunshot to the temple, and called upstairs for an operating room to be readied for a doctor to operate on the second policeman. Sergeant Kelly phoned the station and alerted the shift sergeant that their 'John Doe', a.k.a. George Kitchen, a.k.a. Guido Kiefer, a.k.a. Gerald Keeper was now an escapee from custody, on the loose with an officer's gun, and now wanted for the murder of at least one New Haven police officer. He also got the lead FBI agent's name from the bulletin in his hand and told the shift sergeant to phone the FBI office in Hartford and alert them.

Sergeant Kelly had lost many friends during the Viet Nam war, and a couple more during his years of police service, but today was a new sickening feeling in his gut upon seeing the two unmoving officers laying on the floor. He decided to retreat from the room and allow the doctors and nurses to do their work, in hopes of saving at least one life.

Outside the hospital, no one noticed the man in the doctor's white coat walking through the parking lot pushing a button on a car key and watching for some reaction from one of the many parked cars. He moved slowly and seemed to let his left side slide along in a rather peculiar manner. He didn't fit the profile of the many male doctors within the hospital's directory of doctors, but, again, there was a lot of activity inside, and outside, the Yale-New Haven Psychiatric Hospital today.

Finally, when he pushed the button there was a responding 'beep' coming back from a dark green, older model Honda Civic. "Typical," he thought, "a compact foreign car. Hope it has a full tank of gas, at least." The man had earlier shot two uniform police officers, killing one of them instantly, and taken the little money and car keys from the other after removing his service revolver from his holster. He was now about to steal his car and make a hasty exit from the area. He calculated that he could probably drive 30 to 50 miles and then have to trade this car for someone else's to continue his trip north.

Dr. Greybar's medical clinic had received a phone call from the shift sergeant at the police station and put them on notice regarding the arrestee's escape. Both Dr. Greybar and Dr. Walker decided to clear the afternoon's appointments and allow everyone to leave and find safer surroundings. It only involved five appointments which were all very minor levels, so no patient would miss out on any important medical attention.

Dr. Greybar welcomed the 'off hours' and would try to squeeze in several holes of golf before going home to relax and review patients files.

Dr. Walker, on the other hand, had to use the time to look at homes for sale. He has to find a suitable house for his family to move into as he moves them from Rhode Island to Connecticut. His wife, Gerri, and their four children were in the midst of getting everything packed and ready for the movers; they simply needed an address in New Haven where the movers would unload their belongings.

Dr. Walker phoned his realtor to see if there were any houses that they could visit today, and also if his realtor had a house they could rent for a month, or two. Knowing the housing market in New Haven was much like most college towns, in that, there were few, if any, homes for rent. Nowadays, parent would buy, or rent, homes for their college-bound children and then 'flip' the home afterwards when their children graduated, or dropped out of Yale.

Dr. Walker listened to the phone on the other end ring a second time before hearing Adam Sanders answer. Adam is Gerald Walker's new realtor, having replaced Jerry Eldon who moved back to Westport and was now handling commercial real estate properties.

Gerald Walker identified himself and asked Adam about any residences that he could possibly look at this afternoon. Adam responded that he had located a five bedroom, 4 bath home that is available for lease on a month-to-month. Adam also has some other properties that he can show today whenever Dr. Walker is available. They agreed on a time to meet and Adam Sanders gave Dr. Walker the address of the rental house where they will start today's search.

Dr. Walker changed from his white coat and tie into a more casual attire, said his 'good byes' to Amanda and to Dr. Greybar, and told Dr. Greybar about him being off to meet the realtor, and find a house to purchase. He left the clinic for the afternoon.

CHAPTER 3

His shoulder was hurting like hell, and the pain continued to shoot up his neck into the top of his head, as well as shooting down his arm and out the tips of his fingers. He needed to get something for the pain, but he needed to find another car first.

He pulled the stolen Honda Civic into a parking structure near downtown Hartford and began looking around for a likely replacement parked somewhere therein. As he drove from one parking level to another he saw a very well dressed woman, her arms loaded with shopping bags and packages pressing the button on her car key in an attempt to locate her parked auto. He slowed down to watch her walk slowly up the incline of parking level 3 and suddenly the horn and taillights on a newer model Mercedes answered her search. The woman opened the trunk of her auto as George Kitchen pulled the Honda into a vacant parking space just two spaces away from the woman. He grimaced in pain as he exited the Honda and his groans caught the woman's attention.

She had put the final package into the trunk of her car when she heard the groan and turned to see a man grabbing his left shoulder. She asked him if he was okay or was he having a heart attack. "I don't really know," George answered her, "it's a severe pain in my left side. I just need to rest a minute and it should go away."

"That kind of pain is not anything to ignore, sir," she replied. "I can call 9-1-1 for you, if you'd like me to."

"Thank you, but no. That's not necessary, but I would like some aspirin if you happen to have some." He said.

She said she thought she did have some in her purse and turned to sit her purse on the passenger seat to look for them. As she turned back around with the small white bottle of Bufferin in her hand, she was startled to feel the cold, steel muzzle of a police revolver being pressed against her forehead. She hardly had time to react as a single shot rang out and all went dark.

George Kitchen picked up the bottle of Bufferin off the ground and quickly surveyed the entire third level of the parking garage. No one around; no one reacting to the sound of a gunshot. George quickly picked up the woman's car keys, and her purse and put them on the passenger seat of the Mercedes. He then picked up the woman's lifeless body and carried her down two stalls to the open trunk of the Honda Civic. Depositing her in the trunk, he quickly closed the trunk lid and made certain all doors were locked and the windows rolled up fully.

As he settled into the very comfortable leather seats of the Mercedes, he thought to himself, "now this is the way to travel. First class comfort." And, travel he must! It was time for George to put more distance between himself and the State of Connecticut.

Before he left, though, he had to examine the woman's purse and see if he had gotten any other 'goodies', like a credit card or money. As he went into a fine grain leather wallet in the purse his eyes got bigger and bigger. "Bingo!" he wanted to shout, but knew he couldn't. In the wallet he found $ 478.00 in small bills, and seven credit cards. Three of the credit cards were for gasoline companies and the remaining cards were two Visas, a Mastercard and a Platinum American Express. He looked at her driver's license to get her address since he knew every fill-up with gas would ask for the correct zipcode.

Now it was time to travel and see how this car handles. He pulled out of the parking structure onto a city street and headed for the interstate highway. As George headed the Mercedes north on Interstate 91, he smiled at his good fortune and, also, at how well his new car rode. He knew the next five to six hours of driving would be both comfortable, and quick as he pushed the Mercedes' speed up to 70 mph.

George planned on entering Canada under the pretense of going to Montreal to visit relatives, but, in fact would head north east after entering Canada, and head for Sherbrooke, Quebec. He had been to Sherbrooke once with family and knew that he would not stand out in a city of around 160,000 people. He would rest and heal there for a couple days and then move on westward; or, maybe he would try to land a job on an east-bound freighter sailing out into the Atlantic Ocean. Now, with money and credit cards, and a beautiful car to drive, all he needed was time. He relaxed a bit and surveyed the countryside as he kept the Mercedes just a couple miles-per-hour under the posted speed limit. He began to wonder how much of his high school French language he could remember.

Gerald Walker and Adam Sanders were leaving the third home tour of the afternoon, and Dr. Walker was beginning to wonder to himself if they would ever find anything that would be to the liking of his wife, Gerri. He was about to call it a day when Adam received a call on his cell phone and excused himself to talk to the caller. After a few minutes, Adam returned to Dr. Walker saying "we may have found a perfect house for you. I just got a call from a realtor who is about to list a beautiful, custom-built, six bedroom, five and a half bath, home office, and fully finished basement, two story home with large acreage and a guest house. I know it's been a long day, but if you're up to it, we can go look at this last one for today." Gerald Walker sighed slightly to himself and finally said 'okay' to looking at one more house.

With that, both men got into Adam's car and left for the last home tour of the day. Adam sounded much more enthusiastic when he talked about this home than he had on any of the other houses they have looked at. He said that the architect that designed this home, designed it for his sister and her family of six children; all of whom died in a mysterious plane accident in Asia while on a family vacation. The accident wiped out the entire family including the mother and father. After a year of sitting empty, the architect decided to put it on the market and dispose of it.

Adam was busy telling Gerald Walker about the fine, little details and features incorporated into the house as they pulled into the circular driveway. There before them was a grand, sprawling New England 'Ranch style' house with a large porch bordering the front areas, and luscious, well manicured landscaping. It looked, to Gerald Walker, like the exact house he would design, if he was to design his house. He quickly took out his iPhone and began taking pictures of the beautiful front of the house before they walked up the walkway and onto the front porch. The house had the double entry doors that his wife, Gerri, had on her 'wish list' of things, and each door had a large opaque glass section of finely etched glass that was some of the most attractive Gerald had ever seen. Adam Sanders was looking through his notes on his phone and started telling Gerald that the glass panels had been 'saved' from a castle in Austria that was being demolished and brought to the U.S. to be cut and fitted into the entry doors. The doors themselves were made of German dark oak and were around 300 to 350 years old.

Adam punched the code given him by the other realtor into the keybox hanging close by and retrieved the front door key. The two men entered into a large, grand foyer reminiscent of the grand foyers of European castles, or mansions. Everywhere Gerald looked there were things of beauty; carved wood, chandeliers gleaming brightly with crystals and sparkle, woodworking on both the walls and the ceilings, and marble and hardwood floors everywhere. Everything that Gerald saw told him of the expense, and attention to details, that went into this house.

Gerald saw all the bedrooms, bathrooms and other rooms, as well as the home office area. To say that the office was perfect for him would be an understatement. He decided to take out his phone and resume taking photos of everything that he was seeing; better yet, he phoned his wife and had her on 'Facetime' so that he could show her everything first hand.

Dr. Walker's wife, Gerri, was ecstatic about what she was seeing on her iPhone, even though the pictures were sometimes a bit blurry from her husband moving his phone too fast. She liked the master suite and the very large kitchen which Dr. Walker went through very slowly. She like the size and location of each child's bedroom, and even had a couple of their children watching over their Mother's shoulder and arguing about what bedroom was going to be whose bedroom.

After the tour via 'Facetime' with his wife, Gerald Walker decided that it was time for he and Adam Sanders to get down to discussing the 'hard' facts regarding price and such.

He remembered his mother saying to him, as a child, that "anything worth having, is worth paying for." But Gerald Walker knew that was easy for his mother to say, having come from an 'old money' wealthy New England family; it was not as easy when you are a young doctor with a family, medical school debts, and everything else weighing you down. In addition, he was now going to be responsible for keeping the clinic solvent enough to pay the money owed to Dr. Greybar in his retirement.

Gerald had to admit to himself that both he and his wife Gerri loved everything about the house, but the price was not within their 'home buying budget.' Gerald asked Adam Sanders to create an 'offer' sheet at a price well below the asking and just see what the sellers have to say. Adam Sanders agreed to do that and said he would phone Dr. Walker as soon as he heard something back from the seller's realtor.

With that agreement made, the two men parted company as Adam Sanders returned to his office to prepare the offer sheet.

CHAPTER 4

The long line of cars waiting at the Canadian border, and the time that was being used to check each car, made George Kitchen really uneasy. He knew that this region had always been an easy entrance into the Quebec province of Canada, and, now, that was not the case. He strained his neck trying to see as far down the row of vehicles as he could, to no avail. He also knew that if they searched his car and found the woman's purse and credit cards inside, that he would have more explaining to do than he would like.

He saw a couple people walking back down the long line of vehicles coming his direction. Believing one of them could be a truck driver, he rolled down the driver's side window and asked the fellow if he knew what the problem was.

"Don't know, exactly," the man answered, "seems both U.S. and Canadian officials are looking for some escaped person. Told them I had a 'reefer' stuck in this mess and all the frozen cargo would spoil soon. They don't seem to give a damn, much. Guess I'll call my dispatcher and give him the great news."

George thanked the man for the update and wished him good luck with his load of frozen cargo.

George also started thinking quickly about different

scenarios of how this could play out. He thought about how many rounds of ammo he had in the stolen police revolver. He figured that the worst thing was that he would end up in a shoot-out with both U.S. and Canadian border officials. As he watched the long line of vehicles move forward almost a full car length, he saw an off ramp ahead which led off to an Exxon gas station. He decided he would stop there whether the Mercedes needed gas or not. Gas? He thought he had better check the owner's manual to see if this model used gasoline or diesel fuel, before he created a very bad situation for himself, and for his stolen car.

It took nearly fifteen minutes before he was close enough to the exit to steer the Mercedes for the station, and some time to think and plan. He parked off to the left and somewhat behind the station and its' flow of people. He got out and checked the inside of the filler cap and found the manufacturer's tag which called out for 92+ octane gasoline. One question answered.

As he studied the area, George saw what could be a driveway at the back of the station's lot. It has two cement strips about the width of auto tires and went away from the Exxon station for about twenty to thirty feet before becoming dirt ruts. Then it seemed to lead off through a small forest of trees to somewhere east of where he was now. Given the options of sitting still and perhaps being identified by someone going into or out of the Exxon station, or having a U.S. Border guard spot him and phone for reinforcements, or driving off down an unknown pathway into an unknown forested area, it seemed to George that the forested area and the unknown parts beyond would be the best bet.

He checked his gas gauge and saw he still had more than three-quarters of a tank of gas, so filling up before leaving was not a necessity. He double checked the women's wallet to make certain it was still handy, and was reaching under the driver's seat to check the pistol when a loud rap on the driver's side window occurred. George, startled beyond words, jumped and whipped his head to his left to see a young man in a service station uniform standing outside his car.

George reached for the power window button and lowered his window about six inches and asked the young man if he could help him.

"These parking spaces are for customers only, sir, no all day parking allowed. You'll have to move it!" was the young man's reply.

"Sorry," George answered, "I just stopped long enough to take some medication. I'll be leaving right away." With that response, the young man turned to walk back to the station's office. George knew that the young fellow's coming out to speak to him meant that the station had surveillance cameras and that other people inside the station's office were watching. It also meant that George had been caught on video; not something that he wanted to happen.

George started the engine of the Mercedes, and pointed the distinctive MB emblem on the hood of the car toward the mystery road and into the trees. He needed to get as many miles between him and this Exxon station as he could; as quickly as he could.

The roadway ended quickly and became two ruts which led George through a grove of about a hundred sugar pine trees and into the driveway of a somewhat rustic, outdoorsy, cabin home. Not wanting to attract any more attention George did not slow down at all, but continued on past the cabin in hopes that he would find a state highway, or at least a paved county road which would take him south away from the border guards.

The road became more and more of an endurance test because of the deeper, and deeper, ruts that he was encountering. He began to wonder if he would end up being killed by this road and by it shaking him to death, or by a fatal gunshot from a policeman's gun. After about twenty to thirty minutes of what George considered 'off-roading', he came upon a paved road which left him the option of either turning left, or right. He wasn't sure exactly where he was at, so he opted for left, and an easterly route; perhaps he could find another border crossing before reaching the Atlantic Ocean.

It took George two days of driving back roads, and hunting trails before he reached highway 114. He knew that this highway was a popular route to Quebec province and that both the U.S. and Canada had large, fully manned border inspection stations. He expected that both sides of the border would be on the look out for him, and possible other wanted persons.

George decided to stop at JJ Gas and refill the tank of the Mercedes before doing anything else. Difficult to out run any pursuers without fuel in the tank. JJ Gas is a small, four tank remote gas station at the junction of where New Hampshire state highway 114 and Canadian highway 147 meet before the U.S. and Canadian border. Highway 114 veers off to the right and heads east towards Maine and the tiny town of Canaan, Vermont.

George was not interested in sightseeing anything new; he was tired, hungry, needed a hot shower and a change of clothes. He also had to get rid of his prized Mercedes and plan how he would avoid being captured by the police or federal authorities. He knew that he should not use any of the woman's credit cards, but his stash of cash was not able to provide everything that he was in need of. He ended the gas fill-up at twenty dollars and paid cash to the attendant. He crossed highway 114 on Nelson Road until he could head west on Baumann Road. George continued on Baumann Road until it ended and turned around to head back to a somewhat deserted farmhouse he had passed.

As he pulled the car into the dirt and gravel driveway, a man came out of the house carrying a shotgun. As the man came down each step toward the ground, the barrel end of the gun came higher and higher until it was right at eye level with George's head.

"Don't bother turning the engine off, you ain't stayin'" the man said to George. He looked as though he knew well how to use the double-barrel shotgun, and would demonstrate his expertise willingly. George was uncertain how to react to the man's instructions, so he let the engine continue to run while he rolled his window down.

"Good day, sir," George said. "I'm not here to do you harm. I'm trying to find my way to Canaan, and then on to Hanover, Maine. I got lost and turned around and hoped that some kind person familiar with the area could point me in the right direction."

With that, the man lowered his shotgun so it pointed down toward the ground and said that the locals have been bothered a lot lately with people driving onto their property in big, fancy, foreign cars and bothering them about selling their farms. He called them 'big company land grabbers' and said that local farm owners have started greeting strangers with guns in hand to get their point across about not being interested in selling their lands.

George apologized, again, and said that the Mercedes was actually his wife's car and that his Ford was in the shop.

The man welcomed George onto his property and invited him into his house so that he could draw George a map on how to get to Hanover. The man turned to go back up the steps to his porch as George carefully reached under his seat and felt for his gun. He was reassured when his hand felt the cold steel barrel of the gun and George opened his car door to exit. He was able to tuck the gun into the back belted area of his pants and cover it with the tail of his shirt.

George stood and stretched for a moment before following the man across the porch and into his house. The man offered George a glass of water as he got a tablet and pencil from out of a kitchen drawer. He then proceeded to draw a crude map showing road by names, and not the highway number designations, and pointing out landmarks where George should turn left or right.

George thanked him when he finished the map and offered George a refill on his glass of water.

"I'm a Chevy man, myself, but dem Fords got pretty good lately. Not as good as any Chevy, but better" the farmer told George apparently wanting to have a little conversation with someone who dropped by. "Yep, Fords is better, better than dem ferrin Hondas and such. Born to Chevies, stayin' with Chevies" the man continued.

"What kind of Chevy products do you own?" George asked him, after finishing his second glass of water.

The man explained that he owned two Chevrolet pickup trucks and had just bought his wife a brand new Chevy Impala sedan, which he called their 'Bridge club' and 'goin' to church on Sunday' car. He said that the Impala had just been delivered to him yesterday and his wife, who was visiting her very ill father in Manchester and would not see it until she returned next week.

George told the man how nice that sounded and what a great husband he was for having such a surprise waiting for her return. The two men talked about the map, and the local area for a couple more minutes before George thanked him for the directions, map and water and said he still had a lot of driving to do so guessed he had better get on the road.

The farmer turned to put the pencil and tablet back into the drawer where his wife kept them, and to say his 'good byes' to George.

It was the last thing the farmer ever did.

As the farmer laid in a pool of his own blood, his body slightly quivering from muscle contractions, George put his gun back into the belted waist of his pants. A single shot was all he needed to end the conversation and let George get on with his travels.

George pulled the Mercedes into the huge barn at the back of the property, and parked it right next to the brand new, highly polished, Impala with the keys in the ignition. George could tell that this was not a high crime area or the Impala would have been stolen, stripped of parts, and dumped somewhere out of sight.

Before leaving, George loaded up the trunk of the Impala with all available food that he could find; even taking three beers that he found in the farmer's refrigerator. He then decided to treat himself to a hot shower, shave and a good cleaning up before he went searching for clothes that would fit him.

Almost an hour later, after having buried the farmer's body under a stack of hay in the barn, and cleaning up all traces of blood, George cleaned all fingerprints from the Mercedes, removed all traces of ownership, and buried the car under another stack of hay on the opposite side of the barn area. Pleased with how neat and tidy everything was, he decided it was time to head south; south, with hopes of making it back to the Bridgeport, Connecticut area where George had a sister and a brother who might be able to help him disappear.

Having been on the road only about an hour, he had to admit that the Impala, although brand new, did not handle or ride as nicely as the much older Mercedes. But, wheels are wheels, he thought.

CHAPTER 5

Moving day could not be any less fun for Dr. Gerald Walker, and his wife Gerri. Even with the movers doing the vast majority of work, when you have four young children who think everything in life is a game, and work hard at playing games, there is still a lot of stress involved. The children pushed all of their parent's buttons because of the excitement and anxiety that they were feeling. They had all seen their new house already. Each child was getting their own bedroom, which had already undergone decorating to befit it belonging to a boy or a girl, and the large backyard area surely guaranteed them finally getting their pet dog that their parents had long been promising.

While it was usually less than a two hour drive from Providence, Rhode Island to New Haven, with the four children in the family van, it was guaranteed to make the trip FEEL like a five-to-six-hour journey. The kids all had games to occupy themselves with, as well as a favorite movie on the DVD player which could be viewed, and enjoyed, only in the two rear seats.

Regardless of whether it was two hours, or twelve, the trip ended with Dr. Walker pulling the van into the driveway of the new Walker family mansion. The three older children, knowing how to quickly unfasten their seat belts, were springing out of the van almost as soon as it stop moving. Not realizing that they needed a key with which to unlock the front door, they were soon stopped at the front entrance. Gerald and his wife helped the youngest child get free from her car seat, and leisurely walk up the walkway and up onto the front porch. Gerald pretended to have some difficulty with the key and the front door, and this added to the children's stress levels.

The front door opened and all four children ran into the house like they were being shot out of a cannon. One went this way, one went another way, the third child raced up the stairs to the second level, and the bedrooms. The fourth child, uncertain as to which direction to run, simply stopped in the foyer and watched the other three siblings scatter. Not knowing what to do next, the little girl decided to stand in the foyer craning her neck to look upward in amazement of how high it is, and saying "vow." Vow is her way of imitating her mother's word "wow!"

Dr. Walker and his wife strolled through the living room, dining room, and into the kitchen surveying every piece of furniture, and decorative piece, to make certain the movers had placed them correctly. Pleased with the placement of everything, Gerri Walker decided to find her tea pot and put it to work while Dr. Walker walked off to survey his office layout and attempt to find files and papers that would be needed soon.

While the children frolicked and enjoyed the backyard space, and started the conversation about when they could get a pet dog, Gerald and Gerri Walker enjoyed the last of their 'breakfast' tea and discussed the general layout of the furniture in each room. Gerri Walker could already see a couple rooms that she felt would need some rearranging of furniture pieces. She was a stickler for such things as flow of movement, safety for children, and 'Feng shui' harmony for the home; it was one of the reasons that she chose the moving company that did the move. She liked that they guaranteed satisfaction with how they handled every item, and box, and how they arranged the furniture in the new home. Gerri made a note to phone them in the morning and have them come by to help with the rearranging of the furniture.

Gerald Walker loved the atmosphere he felt in his new home office; the quietness, the gentle flow of air when a window was opened, and the general arrangement of office furniture all made him feel very much at ease. He knew he would be getting much of the upcoming work done here at home. This pleased him greatly.

At dinner, that evening, there was non-stop talking about how great the house is, how great each child's room is, and, of course, how great it will be when they get to get their pet dog. Gerald and Gerri Walker just glanced at each other without commenting on the dog topic.

After dinner, everyone gathered in their new 'family room' for a movie and a lot of relaxing. Within an hour two of their children were sound asleep. Gerri picked one child up in her arms while Gerald Walker got the other child and up the stairs they went; to put each child to bed in their new bedrooms.

When they came back downstairs to the family room, Gerald and Gerri found only their oldest son still awake and watching the movie. Gerri woke their daughter up and helped guide her upstairs to her bedroom.

The following morning, Gerald Walker grabbed his briefcase and headed off to the clinic. He was amazed that it only took him 15 minutes to make the drive from home to work. A real treat, he thought to himself. The traffic congestion here in no way compared to the delays he had to endure in Providence, Rhode Island. His travel distance was about the same, but the drive time was less than half. Definitely, a real treat!

Each day's line of patients gave Dr. Walker more, and more reason to think he had made the right move by joining Dr. Greybar's clinic and putting down roots here in New Haven. Not only did he enjoy the practice with Dr. Greybar, but he was now closer to his parents in Huntington, Long Island, and all his siblings who were settling in and around the Westport, and Bridgeport communities.

Now with the new house, new medical practice, all his four children enrolled in an excellent school district, and doing very well, life seemed heading in the right direction for the young Dr. Walker. If he could just get his father to accept that this is the life choice that his youngest son wants, everything would be perfect.

Thinking of his father reminded Gerald Walker that the gathering of the Walker clan would be occurring this weekend in celebration of his father's birthday. It is a Walker family tradition for all the Walker children, and their families, to gather each year in celebration of Mr. Walker's birthday. While the family normally gathered at the senior Walker's estate on Long Island, where Mr. Montgomery Walker would rent the banquet room at his country club, this year the entire Walker clan was gathering in Westport at the recently-purchased Victorian mansion of his sister, Stephanie Hunter, and her novelist husband, Derek.

Gerald suspects that in addition to celebrating his father's birthday, gathering in Westport will allow his parents an opportunity to scout out the area for a new home to be used when his father retires. With more and more of the Walkers living in Connecticut, it makes sense that his parents would look to this area for a 'smaller' home to move into for their retirement years. Gerald, like most of his siblings, could not imagine his parents really 'downsizing', he knew that time was getting closer, and closer, for that, and retirement to happen. He decided that he needed to phone his wife, Gerri, and remind her of the upcoming trip to Westport for the birthday celebration.

With everything else that is going on, perhaps a reminder is needed.

The drive from New Haven to Westport is less than an hour, including the time it takes Dr. Walker to drive from their home near the New Haven Country Club through town and get onto I-95 going south. Most days of the week, when driving through town, Gerald would not encounter many Yale college students. For some reason, this Friday was different; whether it was an upcoming sports event, or what, he didn't know.

Arriving at his sister Stephanie's Victorian mansion was like arriving at the set of a major motion picture being filmed. Gerald's mother had rented two, very large, canopy type tents and had them erected on the front lawn area, as well as some 'bouncy houses' for the younger kids. The entire area was like watching an ant farm, in that it was so busy with caterers rushing about setting out food trays, warmers, drink dispensers and children's snacks. Florists were rushing about setting floral arrangements out as family members were beginning to arrive. The entire area began to take on the look of a wedding reception setup, rather than an elder gentleman's birthday get-together.

Gerald saw his brother Andrew, and his wife Agnes as they pulled into the driveway. Andrew owned one of the largest companies in the country which dealt in precious metals. He seemed to always be just one Xantac away from an ulcer and Gerald always worried about Andrew's lifestyle. As Gerald was talking to Andrew and Agnes about the current world markets for various metals, he saw his brother Carl and wife Carla arrive in Carl's new corporate auto. Carl was a senior vice-president for Citicorp and very well established in the financial world. Carl dealt a lot with large corporate financial matters, as well as financial dealings with major world governments and businesses. Carl's wife, Carla, is a very busy and prominent chemical engineer and researcher and has been involved in the development of many life-saving drugs.

Gerald's other sibling, his sister Andrea, had arrived earlier with her husband Andrew and were both relaxing with a glass of red wine while watching the florists and caterers do their work. Andrea, one of the top physicist in the country and her research biologist husband Andrew, are people who are always living in the very fast lane of life. So they welcomed an opportunity like this to simply sit and watch and talk and contemplate the meaning of everything. Gerald thought that if he came back here in four hours that they may not have moved from where they sat.

Gerald saw his parents coming out of the Victorian house in front of his sister, Stephanie and her husband Derek. He also saw a man dressed in a business suit carrying a couple rolls of blueprints under his arm follow them off the front porch and down the steps. The man shook hands with Mr. Walker and Derek and Stephanie and went off to a car parked in the back of the driveway.

When the children saw their grandparents coming across the vast lawn area toward the tents they starting running toward them; the smaller and younger the child, the faster they tried to run. The older children sort of strolled toward the approaching grandparents with no sense of hurrying about them.

The Walkers hugged and kissed every grandchild, and Mr. Walker even took a football from one of his grandsons and threw him a pass of about fifteen to twenty yards. Mr. Walker then joked with Gerald about needing a doctor to fix his arm that he had just thrown out. Everyone seemed to be in a good mood.

Later in the day, while the adults were sitting around talking, Mr. Walker told the family about their plans to live on the remodeled third floor of Stephanie and Derek's Victorian while a separate house was being built for them on the far, northwest corner of Stephanie's property. They had met earlier in the day with an architect friend of the Walkers who was both designing their new house, and overseeing the remodeling of the third floor living areas. Mrs. Walker was very happy to be returning to her beloved Connecticut where she was born and raised.

The three day weekend affair went by very fast and soon everyone was traveling back to their home towns and businesses. And Mr. Walker was another year older!

CHAPTER 6

Tom Kitchen thanked the customer for all the items he bought at his Ace Hardware store, while the clerk was bagging everything. Tom tried to meet and mix with as many customers in his hardware store as he could knowing the value of personal contact with customers who want to spend money.

What worried Tom was that he had received a coded message very early that morning, and did not know if he should react to it or not. The message simply read "the Albatross is not in season, but Trout will be." To anyone reading this, it would not mean anything significant, but to Tom it meant that his brother George was coming to see him. Tom had heard about the escape of a suspected murderer from a hospital jail ward up in New Haven several days ago. He worried that the escapee might be his brother, Guido Keeper, now being known as George Kitchen. This name, along with a couple others, could not be directly linked to Tom, but any good research student, or police detective, would soon find a lot more than just a link.

What does Tom do about their other siblings; two sisters who were in the immediate area but never in contact with Tom, or each other. Two sisters so far apart and different, and yet, from the same parents.

Tom was distracted by a customer looking at LED lights and needed someone to answer some questions for her. He thought he had better pay attention to business and just wait to see what happens with the "trout."

It took several days before neighbors discovered the dead body of the elder Mrs. Thompson in her rural home. She was not a person to be seen out and about a lot since she sold her beauty shop, and then her barber shop, in town. She liked her semi-retirement, and being able to spend a lot more time with her grand children and her friends at the church's seniors club.

Mrs. Thompson, like many people who retire, just could not get out of the habit of doing people's hair. So when she overheard the stranger asking the waitress at the local diner where a barber shop was located in town, she gave her talents some promoting. The man seemed shy and said that he needed to cut his hair very short and dye it a grey color for a play he was going to be doing in Boston. He even had a picture of the style he needed so she could be certain she could accommodate him.

Mrs. Thompson gave the man her home address and offered to lead him back there so he would not get lost. He took her up on her offer and said he would pull his Impala in behind her car and follow her.

When they arrived at her house, Mrs. Thompson went right to work on the man's hair; trimming it, thinning it out, cutting it into the style in the picture, and, finally, coloring it to a very nice, natural looking, 'salt-and-pepper' grey color that completely changed the man's rough looks. He was amazed with his transformation when Mrs. Thompson finished her magic, and kept complimenting her on what a great job she had done. After talking for several minutes about how to maintain both the style and the color, Mrs. Thompson asked if he wanted a cup of tea. He thanked her very much and said that would be nice. He then asked what he owed her as he reached for his wallet. She finished putting the kettle full of water on her stove and turned to answer his question about money.

She never fully saw the pillow, so nicely needlepointed with "Home Sweet Home" he placed over her face as the kitchen knife was thrust into her abdomen once. Twice. Three times; the third time severed a major artery and Mrs. Thompson felt as though she should just go to sleep. Quiet, peaceful sleep. Darkness, and silence.

The more people that George Kitchen murdered, the better he got at cleaning up the mess that he made in doing so. He had all blood from Mrs. Thompson's body, all his hair from the very nice cut and coloring that she did for him, all her tools and dyes she had used, yes, every single little thing showing any activity at all was gone. A very spotless, no trace job, George thought to himself.

George locked everything up tightly, after hiding her body in a butler's pantry, and started his Impala up to continue his trip to Bridgeport. As he pulled out onto the highway, he looked into the rear view mirror hardly recognizing the person looking back at him. "What a change!" he thought. He suddenly felt more secure in driving back toward cities, and perhaps people, who would have recognized him before his hair coloring and style change.

"One sure way to confirm this change," he told himself, "is to find my siblings and get their reactions." It is a beautiful, warm and sunny day, George thought, a great day for a drive; especially a drive to Bridgeport.

Tom Kitchen loved the computer system that the Ace Hardware group used for sales and inventory replenishment. It certainly helped him know when stocks of good selling items were low and needed to be reordered from the distribution center. He did not like the system when it went down! Down, as in not functioning at all; not functioning as in not able to record each sale, cash drawer opening automatically, making change, and, of course being tied into the system was their credit card acceptance system.

So for four hours Tom's cashiers were busily writing sales on multi-copy sales books, making change the old fashion way, and doing the best to make customers happy and cheerful. Tom knew his crew would do their job, but he found it really surprising how many customers thought that this was the end of the world: no computer system operating in their hardware store!

Finally after lunch hour, Tom got a phone call that the problems with the 'system' had been resolved and everything was back to normal. "Normal?" thought Tom. "Back in operation, maybe, but hardly 'normal.'"

Tom and his assistant manager now had to take all of the morning's sales and re-enter them into the system so that inventory numbers would be correct and stock could automatically be replaced. It was a proven fact that each sale re-entered, took one-and-one-half times longer than entering the sale originally. Let the fun begin! Tom thought as he sat down at his computer terminal.

Two hours later, Tom's iPhone message read "Sale on Now! Trout Season is Open at Phil's Sporting Goods!" Although Tom was not a fresh water fisherman, he knew that trout season was still many months away. This message meant that his brother was at the designated meeting place. Tom had to get another clerk off the floor and have them input the sales information so he could leave and attend a 'meeting.'

Dr. Greybar was very pleased with his decision to bring young Gerald Walker in to his practice and arrange to turn the clinic over to him upon retirement. He liked Gerald as a doctor, even more as a person, and all the patients had really come to like him also. As Dr. Greybar was found of saying, "life is always better when a plan comes together."

So, it seems, this plan has.

Dr. Greybar has started taking Mondays and Fridays off and getting in more rounds of golf. He has even joined up with three friends for a regular Friday tee time and is beginning to enjoy life, and the game of golf, a great deal more. His handicap was starting to drop little by little and he even thought about rejoining the country club where they played. He was also glad that none of his long time patients insisted on seeing him when they came into the clinic; except for Mrs. Fitzpatrick. She liked Dr. Walker, as much as she could like anything, but always wanted to know where Dr. Greybar was at. Dr. Walker usually told her, but kept his answer very short and then changed the subject.

Dr. Walker liked Mrs. Fitzpatrick, in spite of her bitter, crabby personality. He often would find himself talking about his parents and his siblings and their various accomplishments in life. Mrs. Fitzpatrick liked what she felt was the 'special' attention that she was getting from young Dr. Walker and was not really missing Dr. Greybar as much as she let on.

As for Dr. Walker, he was enjoying his new life here in New Haven now, also. The move-in was completed and both he and his wife were able to find everything they went looking for. The kids were enrolled in their schools and adjusting well; their grades were all beginning to come up to where smart children's grades should be. Gerri Walker has found her favorite little stores, a great market and a butcher that she adores, and all the little things a person longs for when relocating to a new city and state. Gerri Walker longed to see her close girl friends she had in Providence, but setting up a new household, getting children enrolled in new schools, and all the myriad of things a head of household must do in a new home town just kept her busy, busy, busy. Gerri knew that one day soon she would venture back to Providence to visit her friends, but for now her family would have to be her friends.

One thing that is making Gerri Walker's transition easier is her connection with the wife of her brother-in-law, Johnny Hamilton. Johnny's wife , Sally Hamilton, and Gerri Walker seemed to hit it off as soon as they met about seven years ago. Sally has 3 children, had worked in a travel agency before the children arrived, and now was a stay-at-home housewife. The two women had more in common with each other than any one could imagine. So when Sally needed some advice, or an opinion on some new product, or such, she phoned Gerri; and, vice-versa with Gerri. There were only chats at Walker family functions, and phone calls two or three times a week. Sally lives in Bridgeport so dropping in for tea is not a reasonable expectation. But Sally and Gerri always had their talks on the phone while they each had a cup of tea at home. Moving closer to her friend Sally was another check on the 'plus side' of relocating to New Haven. In Gerri's life, she was closer to her in-laws than anyone else, having lost both her parents in a plane crash several years before. Gerri's brother and sister were both professionals living in foreign countries and only her sister was apt to phone every once in a while. Her brother would send emails, and had tried to do 'Skype' phone calls, but was not the best person around technology; consequently, the call never was completed. He blamed it on the French internet connections; Gerri thought otherwise.

As far as sporting goods stores went, Phil's was a nice place. Tom was not really into sports so he did not have much appreciation for the wide variety of items on the shelves. Tom knew that his inventory of goods would be nearly triple what a sporting goods store would have to carry, but, as far as sporting goods stores went, this was a nice place. Fishing equipment? Well, he had tried fishing once and kept getting the hook caught on the back of his fishing vest that he had bought just for the trip. After catching the hook in the back of his head and putting a fair size cut into his scalp, he knew fishing would be marked off his 'to do' list.

As Tom looked at the variety of reels on display he heard someone ask him "are you looking to fish for Albatross or Trout?" Tom started to answer 'trout' before turning around, but decided to look at the person connected with the voice.

Tom turned to see a grey haired, curly hair man with a full beard and mustache standing there looking at him. His voice sounded familiar, but he was certain he had not met this man before. He looked as though he could be in his late thirties, early forties, and the more Tom looked into his eyes the more familiar he seemed to Tom.

"Why would anyone go fishing for Albatross?" Tom asked the man.

"Someone has to like Albatross, but no one in this house," the man answered.

Tom stood staring at the man and began to understand more and more. "Sometimes the house has lots of fish, other times we go fishing."

The man turned several times to look around the store to see if people were close by before saying, "but the house has to have a key, even when it's out of fish. Do you have the key?"

With that, Tom grabbed the man in a huge bear hug which he ended quickly before anyone in the store saw them. "I did not recognized you, Gil. What a difference you've made in your appearance," Tom told the man. He hardly believed that the man standing just two feet in front of him was his brother, George.

"I had to. I have too many people looking for the old me, including various police departments, NSA agents, state police, and the FBI. I have been running for a while and need to get moving again. Do you still have the key?" Guido, or George, asked Tom.

"I still have the big key, but the minnow has the rest of the keys." Tom told George. Tom knew that if anyone was within hearing distance, that this conversation would not make any sense to them. That was the point: the coded messages had been arranged years ago when all four children were much younger. Coded, so that anyone other than the siblings would have no idea of what was being discussed.

"I'll have to find a minnow and check on that, but, we also have to fish together." George remarked.

The two men decided that they had been in the same spots talking too long and had to relocate. There were several set locations where various siblings would meet and talk and they all knew the coded messages giving the locations. "They're not catching minnows, or trout, by the long place, but they could still be very hungry," George said as the two men turned to walk out of the sporting goods store at different times.

Tom knew that he would be meeting his brother, George, at the food truck location just south of the Long Wharf Pier in New Haven Bay in one hour. This is what the last conversation between the two men really meant.

Long Wharf Pier is exactly that; a long pier jutting out into New Haven Bay which is surrounded by a park and public areas. It is also the home of several food trucks and a good place to meet in public. It is also a place visited by police officers on patrol around lunch time; so Tom and George would need to be very careful and watchful.

While not on a par with some other cities food trucks, like Portland or Los Angeles, New Haven does have a nice variety and caters to the college crowd. Tom and George made their choices, got their food and sat down at a picnic table far away from the gathering crowd at the trucks.

"You know HE is going to catch us one day," George said to Tom. "He's getting closer and closer all the time and we need to gather all our evidence and get it into a new safe place." Tom agreed with his brother but still did not feel the concern for safe keeping that George was feeling. "The minnow has a lot of safety in the sky," Tom said as he watched George devour his plate of Barbeque food.

"The minnow has a spouse that is interested in many, many things and could well discover the safety in the sky." George answered back. "It's time to gather things and move on. Move before HE finds any of us, and begins his retribution on all of us. You know he HAS to, and HE knows he has to, so it is only a matter of time."

Again, Tom agreed with his older brother, but lacked the same sense of urgency that he felt.

The two men sat eating their lunch and watching the college students, and office workers from the nearby companies, place their food orders at the various trucks. Tom counted eleven trucks which seemed to him to be six or seven fewer than were normally here.

Just as Tom watched two college girls flirt with some men at a Mexican food truck, he saw two police officers get out of a black & white squad car. "George, slowly, without looking toward the street, turn around and look at the bay. Watch boats or something out there. Two uniforms just got out of their patrol car and are heading for the Argentinian food truck. Stay calm, move slowly."

Tom hated to not be able to look around and watch the two cops, but he knew he had better admire some boats on the water. He slowly scooted around until he faced due east and was actually watching three sailboats on the bay. He watched them for what seemed to be an hour, but was actually only eight minutes. He then asked Tom if they were still there, to which Tom answered "yes." This bothered George: this not being aware of his surroundings, and not be in charge of his plan of action. This was really bothering George. He looked off to his right and saw only the rest of the Long Warf Park stretching out toward City Point and the entrance to the Winter Harbor area. With families walking dogs and children running and riding bikes, George knew he had no escape that direction. He watched several kids running around before looking off to his left and toward the mouth of the Mill River, the I-95 bridge crossing, and the docks and storage tanks for oil and gas. A couple tankers were at harbor and he wondered if he could get a job as a deck hand on one of them.

The longer George sat, the more uneasy he became; he wanted to get up and move out of this park and this whole area, but he knew Tom was watching.

Finally, after eating their food for about twenty minutes, the two patrolmen jumped up and ran to their patrol car. Rapidly getting into the car, they sped away with their red & blue lights flashing. As they got a quarter mile away on Long Wharf Drive, they hit the siren to signal to everyone that they were now in a hurry. Once they were around the bend and out of sight, both Tom and George let out a long, quiet sigh of relief.

Tom looked at George and said, "plan B now and I'll see the minnow in a few days. I maintain her grandfather clock and I know when her husband is working so we can have some privacy. You leave now, I'll go the other way."

George hesitated and surveyed the park surroundings before saying "okay, plan B, you to minnow. Stay safe."

The two brothers went their separate ways. George, or Gilbert if you prefer, pocketed the money that Tom had given him and felt better about being able to sleep inside tonight. George had decided to drive up I-95 toward New

London and get a room at an Extended Stay America where he could cook his own meals and stay more secluded until he was contacted next.

George stopped at a major supermarket and bought groceries for him to prepare each day. He bought what he thought would last for twelve or thirteen days, and paid in cash. For his room at the Extended Stay, he used a credit card issued to Ace Hardware which Tom had given him so that he would not arouse any suspicions by a nosey desk clerk.

Once inside his new home of a room, George relaxed and decided to go buy some different clothes in town tomorrow. For his other essentials, he walked over to the coin operated laundry and did a wash and dry.

After finishing his washing, and eating dinner, George turned on the TV to get the evening local news. He was very surprised when he heard about a farmer found shot to death near the small farming community of Norton, New Hampshire. No clues or suspects were available at broadcast time, but state police suspect that the person, or persons, responsible have fled into Canada since Norton is within a few miles of the U.S. & Canadian border. "Good" George thought to himself, "keep thinking that."

George then decided to find a movie to watch until falling asleep. He selected something relaxing: "Texas Chainsaw Massacre."

CHAPTER 7

"This goes beyond being strange," Gerri thought to herself. She would get herself put together, her youngest child ready to be taken to pre-school learning center, and then she would phone Sally Hamilton again, for the "umpteenth" time. Gerri had been trying to reach Sally and had only been able to leave messages; messages left on their voicemail at home for weeks now. Maybe it was time to call another family member and see if Sally and Johnny had taken an extended vacation, which didn't seem right especially with their three kids in school, or if something had happened to Johnny.

As Gerri stood in her kitchen holding the phone in her hand, she debated with herself: Sally or Stephanie? Maybe, just maybe, she could reach Carla easier than Stephanie. Debate over, she would try Sally Hamilton first.

The phone rang and went immediately to voicemail. Very strange, Gerri thought, very strange. She redialed the number only to have it do the same thing, again. Well, she decided, she would reach out to Carla first and see if she might know what was happening at the Hamilton household. She dialed the phone number she had for Carla's cell phone expecting it to go to her voicemail, but, to Gerri's surprise, Carla answered.

"Hi, Carla, it's Gerri Walker. I hope I'm not calling at a bad time, but I have been trying to reach Sally Hamilton for weeks now and have not been able to. Do you know if she and Johnny may have taken a vacation, or are on a trip somewhere?"

Gerri listened as Carla started answering her questions after saying how nice it was to hear from her. Carla asked how Gerri's children are and if she and Gerald are completely moved in yet, or not. Carla talked about several things, and asked questions of Gerri, but never seemed to get around to answering Gerri's initial question: do you know if Sally and Johnny have taken a vacation, or not?

Finally, Gerri interrupted Carla and asked her "what's wrong, Carla? You're not answering my question. Is there something wrong with Sally? Or Johnny?" As Gerri listened to Carla, all she could say was "OH, MY GOD! Oh my God!" Gerri listened intently for a couple minutes before beginning to speak.

"Do they know if she's going to live, or not? She asked. The more information she got from Carla, the more she wanted to just start crying. She suddenly felt lost and unable to do anything, at all, for her best friend. She listened to all of the details of how the auto versus pickup truck accident had occurred, the condition of the two surviving children, and how quickly Sally and Johnny's eight year old son had been taken. Gerri listened, and listened. Carla told her that her sister-in-law, Andrea Stevens, had tried to contact her through her cell phone number but got a message that the number was no longer in service. Andrea was supposed to have called Gerald, but she didn't know if she ever did. Gerri was certain that if her husband had gotten news of this type that he would have said something to her. She listened and talked for a long time with Carla, and suddenly became aware that she had to walk down to the corner to meet her little girl as she got off the school bus. If she was not there, the bus driver would keep her on the bus and she would return to the school.

Gerri quickly explained this. having to meet her daughter, and asked Carla if she could call her back in a little while. Carla explained that she and Carl were staying at Johnny's house to help him, and if she wanted to call there that would be fine.

Gerri grabbed her purse as she bolted out the door and headed for the school bus rendezvous.

Tom Kitchen was making a regular visit to his customer's home; a visit which had been planned months ago. Besides owning the Ace Hardware store in town, Tom also owned several other business, one of which is a clock store known as "About Time." Tom has always liked tinkering with clocks and had become quite the expert, especially on many makes and models of grandfather-type clocks. He was informally know around town as the 'keeper of all time' because of his ability to fix almost all clock problems. He preferred that title rather than being referred to as 'the keeper of the key,' Another title acquired from his making all the keys at his hardware store.

As he drove down the street, he saw the new Chief of Staff from the, soon-to-be-dedicated, children's hospital. He did not want to run into her, so he slowed his van and pulled over to the curb and parked. He watched as she started her car and drove off in the opposite direction. He felt safe in making his house call now except as he got closer to the house there were several other cars that he did not recognize parked in front, and in the driveway. Again Tom parked his van and sat and watched.

After twenty minutes, or so, a couple from the house next door went over to the house Tom was watching with some food dishes, and some bottles of wine. Tom was beginning to think that this was not the right time for him to make a house call and see the minnow.

Tom would wait until another time when there was not any foot traffic at his sister's house to stop by and service her clock. He checked for traffic and did an unconventional U-turn and headed the van back the direction he had come from.

He would return to the hardware store and see if he had made any money today, or if there are any problems for him to straighten out; then he might try to reach out to the 'trout' to see how he is doing.

Dr. Walker could not believe what he was hearing on the phone call from his wife. How could Sally be near death in the hospital, one of her sons dead, and another son and a daughter barely hanging onto life? This certainly did not make sense and he told Gerri that he would call the hospital in Bridgeport and talk to the doctor overseeing her case. He would get more news, but in the meantime, he had to phone his brothers and sisters and find out what was happening, and what HAD happened. So he told Gerri he would phone her back shortly after he talked to Carl or Carla.

Finishing the call with his wife, Dr. Walker asked Dr. Greybar if he would mind seeing the next patient who was just coming in to get a flu shot. He explained that he had to make some emergency personal phone calls. He closed the door to his office and began calling Walker family members. He talked to Stephanie first, and she told him everything that she knew that had happened: young man, heavily intoxicated hits young man on bike, gets distracted and accelerates pickup into driver's side of Sally's van with her and all three kids inside. Gerald Walker asked a number of questions about the young man who hit Sally and about the two surviving children. Finally, Gerald asked how Johnny was handling the whole event. Stephanie said that he was spending a lot of time at the hospital, and that he accepted a new position with Carl Walker's employer, Citicorp. She thought, all in all, Johnny was doing okay, but didn't know how long he could keep it together. Stephanie suggested that Gerald call Carl or Carla as they were seeing Johnny most, and spending a lot of time with him at his house. Gerald thought that was a good suggestion and said he would do so. Gerald asked about Stephanie's husband, Derek, and his latest novels. After a few minutes he told Stephanie that he had to call the doctor attending to Sally at the hospital and get a medical update.

Gerald phoned the hospital and after playing the fifty question game with nurses and receptionists, was able to be connected with a Dr. Chambers. After introducing himself to Dr. Chambers, he told him why he was calling and what he wanted to know.

It took about ten minutes for the two doctors to completely discuss Sally's vitals and prognosis, and another four minutes to find out that the two doctors had met briefly about four years ago at an ABFM conference. The American Board of Family Medicine (ABFM) holds conferences for doctors certified in, and specializing in, the practice of family medicine. Dr. Chambers was one of several guest speakers, and Dr. Walker, who was living in Providence, RI and was part of the host city's committee, met and talked about how well the conference was being handled. Dr. Chambers remembered the meeting much better that Gerald Walker did.

Unfortunately, Gerald Walker was not very optimistic

about Sally's improving after hearing the information that Dr. Chambers had. Although, miracles had happened before, this would be equal to a miracle and three-quarters.

After digesting the information that Dr. Chambers had given him, Gerald phoned Carl to check up on Johnny Hamilton. Carl has always liked Johnny Hamilton since they first met when he started dating Johnny's sister in college. Later, after Johnny had gone to work for the 1st Trust & Savings Bank group, and Carl had become a vice president with Citicorp, Carl had wished that Johnny would dislike his job with 1st Trust enough that Carl could lure him away and hire him into the Citibank division. They had always remained close friends and never talked "shop" with each other to keep their two financial worlds separate.

Carl answered his cell phone on the fourth ring and was delighted to hear Gerald's voice at the other end. They skipped the updating and pleasantries and got right to the accident, the condition of the two remaining children, Sally's current condition, and how Johnny is holding up under all the stress. Carl and Gerald talked for nearly a half hour, non-stop, before Gerald asked Carl what he or Gerri could do for Johnny or the family.

Carl was silent for a few seconds before answering Gerald with, "pray. Go to church and light a candle and pray a lot. As you have told me, after talking to Dr. Chambers, there is nothing positive about Sally's condition, and her prognosis is grim. Just pray. I'll give you or Gerri a call on your cell if I think of anything that is needed."

With that, Gerald ended the call and leaned back in his office chair for a moment to think about what he had heard.

It was four days before Tom Kitchen connected with the 'trout', and found out that he was starting to get a 'little stir crazy.' He started complaining as soon as Tom said "hello", and never stopped until Tom felt he had heard enough and told George so. He figured that the situation was not optimum for George, but George did not have a lot of options; he had killed a cop, a farmer, an innocent female shopper, and who knows how many others. So his position was not one of being able to move around very much in public. He might not like his surroundings, but he would not like prison either. Tom tried to calm George down and explain the situation to him in plain and simple terms.

George listened to what Tom was telling him, but still did not calm down. He wanted to gather some things he felt were very important, move them to a new location and then head for Mexico. Mexico is a country that he could live in and feel relatively safe from prosecution; and his fluent Spanish language abilities would certainly be an asset. Tom understood his boredom and edginess with seeing only the same four walls every hour of every day, but murdered bodies were starting to be found, and reports of stolen autos were being made public. One of those bodies belonged to a known criminal named Jesus Mendoza.

Jesus has been arrested more times than Famous Amos has baked cookies, says George, who heard about Jesus from another Mendoza family member while in jail. It seems the Mendoza Mob is a known crime family specializing in everything illegal. Jesus's segment of crime involved drugs, false identities, getaway autos, and guns. Nothing that Jesus Mendoza touched ever turned out to be legal. Nothing.

But George did not have to worry about that, he met Jesus to buy a couple untraceable guns, and arrange for a car that would not be sought after by law enforcement. Jesus sensed that George was looking for things that he could not pay for and called him on it. That was Jesus's second mistake that morning; his first was only having one body guard with him for protection. George's temper was under control until the point that Jesus demanded to see money first before producing any guns, ammo, or cars.

That brings up Jesus's third mistake: not thinking that George already HAD a gun and would not be prone to use it. If nothing else, George had become a person who conserves; ammo, that is. With only three bullets left in the stolen police pistol, he put a shot through the heart of Jesus's body guard, a second bullet through his head, and a single bullet through the forehead of Jesus. George stood there and looked at the two dead bodies, quivering with muscle spasms and bleeding out all over the floor, and thought to himself that he needed to do his business, next time, with ONE bullet each. Now he was out of ammunition and had to steal more guns. "Oh, well," he thought to himself, "maybe I'll do better next time."

George used Jesus's equipment to make a false driver's license, phony credit cards, auto registration and insurance card for a car he selected, and then helped himself to four guns, including the ones on the body guard's body and Jesus's body, and two extras. He also found an envelope of money in Jesus's desk drawer which he helped himself to, and cleaned up the entire room where the killings occurred.

This all occurred before making his connection with his brother Tom. So now George was stuck in a small room with not much to occupy his time, worrying about whether, or not, he may have left a trace of something tying the killings to him. The Mendoza Mob has resources far beyond those of George; and, far beyond those of Tom, also.

Tom reminded George of all of this while talking to him on the phone, but George argued that his changed appearance would throw the police off. He was only worried about the Mendoza Mob and what revenge they would seek. Tom kept trying to drive the same point home: stay inside and you stay safe. George listened, thought about what he was hearing, and knew his thoughts were much different.

CHAPTER 8

Dr. Walker had gotten the news a couple days earlier that the brand new, multi-million-dollar, highly-technologically based, children's hospital in Bridgeport was going to be dedicated this coming weekend. It is to be named after Dr. Walker's parents as the 'Montgomery & Eloise Walker Children's Medical Center.' It is a great honor for his parents, and well deserved, as they have long been supporters of better medical facilities for children and have contributed millions of dollars to the improvement of this facility over the years.

He rearranged his appointment schedule so that he and his family could take two days off and stay in Bridgeport to visit with the family after the dedication ceremonies. It would give Gerri a chance to catch up on 'family events', and the children could run and play with their cousins. It would also give Gerald an opportunity to talk with Johnny about his wife, Sally. He certainly was not looking forward to this type of talk, especially with a family member, but he knew he had to have the talk to help Johnny prepare for the event that Gerald knows is coming in the very near future: Sally's death.

Saturday, the dedication day for the new wings of the hospital, turned out to be as near perfect as the local weatherman had promised. Blue skies and a few puffy white clouds were the only interruptions to a steady stream of warm sunshine falling upon every person.

Dr. Walker was immediately impressed by the architectural styling used for the two new children's wings. The project architects brought together a classic style with modern materials and produced a neo-classic design that will look new for many, many years. As he talked to some of the staff, Dr. Walker became more impressed with what the hospital contained, especially in the ware of technology. Every area of every floor had robotic nurses which are brightly colored computerized robots that the children can interact with, and not be afraid of. The hospital also has an app which was developed for parents and doctors to communicate with each other in real time, as well as an email system that allows emails to go back and forth via smart phones in real time. Technology is certainly a big part of the operation of the new children's hospital wards.

To Dr. Walker, though, one of the most interesting things he found is that the hospital directors were able to lure a renowned pediatric surgeon away from Mt. Sinai Hospital in New York to join this hospital as the Chief of Staff for the children's hospital. Dr. Helen Eldon is well known and highly regarded in the area of children's medicine and is originally from the Bridgeport area. Gerald Walker met Dr. Eldon when he did his 'rounds' as a young intern years ago, and was instantly impressed by her knowledge of pediatric medicine. He felt that someone on the Board had done a fantastic job in luring her here to

Bridgeport. With what Dr. Walker knows of her expertise, he felt that the operating, and staffing of the hospital, is being given to very capable hands.

The actual dedication ceremony for the Montgomery & Eloise Walker Children's Medical Center was grand and lengthy. Every dignitary seemed to have long speeches prepared, except for Mr. & Mrs. Walker. They simply said that they were fortunate to have had a life good enough to be able to share what they have with children who are in need. A very prestigious part of the ceremony was reserved for the state Governor who presented a "Great Humanitarian Award" to the Walkers for funding the new hospital wings.

After the ceremonies concluded, a catered lunch was served under a huge tent set up on the open lawn area between the two main hospitals. All of the Walker family members were present, as well as members of the state legislature, Mr. Walker's country club friends, and many members of the medical profession. It was like a "Who's Who" of prominent New England society and medical people. In an area largely over shadowed by events in New York City, and elsewhere, the hospital's dedication of new pediatric wings was a big event. Area TV stations covered the dedication ceremonies, and following luncheon, and even a reporting team from CNN had been given a press pass.

Gerald Walker seemed to migrate, quite naturally, to a group of doctors and pediatric specialists during lunch, while Gerri Walker lunched with their children and the other members of the Walker family. Gerald loved being able to learn about the new technology that the brand new hospital contained, and how every thing comes together for the benefit of children who need it. Every doctor, and RN, who would be working with Dr. Eldon, the new Chief of Staff, had only the highest of praise for her and her ability to get important things accomplished. The more Dr. Walker listened and talked with the other doctors, the more impressed he became with both the new pediatric wings, and with Dr. Helen Eldon, the new Chief of Staff. He found ideas and practices that he felt would benefit some of his own younger patients in his practice back in New Haven. He so enjoyed being with, and talking 'shop' with, the various doctors of the new pediatric wards that he nearly forgot about his wife and children. He knew that it was time for him to join his wife and return to the Walker family gathering.

Bidding 'farewell' to all the pediatricians, Dr. Walker found his way quickly back to the Walker family table which had been set up with extra empty seats, just in case someone else was invited to sit with the family. Gerald Walker dropped right into a conversation with Gerri, Mrs. Walker and Stephanie about how high college tuition costs are now, versus how much higher they may be when Gerri's four children are ready to enroll. Mrs. Walker, whose parents had sent her to Wellesley College near Boston, had no concept of the cost involved with educating children, and found the discussion very 'eye-opening.' As she listened to the discussion go back and forth about various suitable colleges, and their related costs, she thought about discussing with her husband setting up some small 'college fund accounts' for each of their grandchildren. Mrs. Walker was pretty certain that he would be in favor of it. If not, she would convince him otherwise. Mrs. Walker made a mental note to discuss this type of account with Johnny Hamilton, as this is his area of expertise, and he could give her good advice on how to proceed.

As Gerald listened to the discussion about college costs, he watched the children all running and laughing and very much into a game of 'hide-and-seek.' Gerald liked the energy level of all the children and was very willing to get involved in their game when asked to by one of his children. The problem with playing this particular game in this location was that there was a deficiency of natural hiding places. So the game became less, and less hiding, and consequently, less-and-less seeking. Gerald could understand the children's desire to end the game about thirty minutes later, and head for more food and beverages.

Gerald walked back toward the family's table as he watched his children grab some lemonade and get into their chairs for more lunch. One thing Gerald knew for certain, was that growing children, at play, can burn up food calories rapidly; and, he knew his children had.

After eating more lunch, and having their fill of lemonade, the children headed off to join other children in a game of tag. This time Gerald declined his children's offer for him to join the running and tagging, saying that he had to talk to the adults for a few minutes. What he really wanted was to simply relax for a few minutes and catch up on his sibling's lives. Gerald and Gerri always seem to hear about something which affected a family member last; long after everyone else heard about it.

The conversations among the family members went on for another hour before Mr. Walker announced that he rented the banquet room at the Brooklawn Country Club for an informal, relaxing, dinner for the family members. He did not believe that the evening would run very late, after watching the children running and playing for the last couple hours. So, as the events of the day started winding down, the Walker family gathered their children, and belongings and headed for the country club.

As they drove to the country club, Gerald and Gerri were conversing with each other about news learned from various family members. The main story, of course, was the auto accident involving Sally Hamilton and her children. Gerri was almost beyond words with the damage that Sally, and her two surviving children, had sustained as a result of the collision. Gerald had a better medical understanding about their conditions, and prognosis, after talking to Dr. Chambers and other doctors familiar with their cases. He would have to be careful in giving Gerri too much information about her good friend, Sally Hamilton. He felt that it would be better to give her enough information so that she understood the gravity of their conditions, but not enough to cloud her sense of optimism. He knew it would be important for his wife to hold out hope for her friend's recovery.

The banquet room was very elegant, and the dinner was delicious and enjoyable. All the children had spent their supply of energy earlier in the day, so they all were content to watch TV and eat their dinner. The adults talked among themselves about a myriad of topics as though they all had never had the opportunity to talk with each other before. Mr. Walker informed the family that he and Mrs. Walker had sold the estate in Huntington, L.I., and were currently staying with Derek and Stephanie in Westport until a house under construction on their property was finished. Then they would move from the third floor of the Victorian, over to the newly constructed house on the northwest corner of Stephanie's property.

Mr. Walker also told the family that he had finally retired from the financial firm that he had help found, and would continue on as a paid member of the Board of directors. He also told everyone that he and Mrs. Walker would be taking a trans-Atlantic cruise, and would be staying in London for a few weeks with friends while the contractors were finishing the remodeling of the third floor of Derek and Stephanie's Victorian. The entire family thought the news was all good and welcomed the retirement of Mr. Walker who had been known for many years to have worked too hard, and too long.

With the dedication ceremonies behind them, and the family dinners and meetings over with, Gerald made one more visit to the hospital to get an update on Sally's, and her children's, conditions before getting his family into their van and headed home to New Haven. The updated news about Sally was not encouraging, and Gerald would have to figure out how best to filter the information so that he could update his wife about her friend. He did not like the idea of not telling his wife, Gerri, all the latest information about her friend, but he knew, too well, that telling her about the reoccurring problems would only bring stress to his wife, and doubt about Sally's ability to make a recovery.

He waited until they had gotten home and the children were busy playing outside to tell Gerri about Sally Hamilton. He did include a little information about some of the problems the doctors were having, but left the major problems unsaid. It seemed to be enough information for Gerri to continue to be optimistic about her friend Sally, and to keep praying for her recovery. Dr. Gerald decided that his next project would be to review some patient's files.

By now the room at the Extended Stay America was beginning to feel as though it was about four feet by four feet, and George was really stressing out about the closeness of the four walls. Not being a person who likes small places, even as a child, he kept telling himself to think about how small and confining a prison cell would feel. He kept telling himself that, but it didn't help to make his hotel room feel larger. He was pretty much going through the same routine every day; day-after-day-after-day. George couldn't decide if it was his lack of mobility, or the tedium of repeating the same things over and over. He had seen every movie available, every program shown on HGTV, every news program broadcasted, and an entire plethora of other, less interesting, programs. It has been nine days since he checked into the hotel, and it felt like nine months; nine long, very long days. Days that did not allow him to venture outside and enjoy bright sunshine and calming breezes.

Finally, out of desperation, he phoned his brother on the cellphone to let him know that he was going for a short walk. Short walk, not a lengthy hike, just a short walk. Outside.

"No!" answered Tom when he heard of George's intentions. "Stay put! The 'minnow' is in critical condition in the hospital as a result of being T-boned by a drunk driver. She may not live, and one of her children died in the crash. The cops are watching everywhere, and everyone.

You have to be inside and safe or we're all in jeopardy!" Tom sounded madder, and more stressed than he ever had before, but Tom was not the one having to do the same things over, and over, and live within what feels like a coat closet size of a room. Tom isn't being pursued by both state and federal officials, as well as the Mendoza Mob. Tom has freedom; George has confinement.

There's that word, again: confinement. Think, George told himself, think about confinement. Think about how much smaller that prison cell, that they have waiting for you, will feel. Think about how many Mendoza family members are probably in that same prison waiting for instructions from the outside as to how many pieces they should cut you into. Think about all these things and just sit tight. George let out a long, slow sigh and told his brother Tom that he would sit still. Sit and wait. Some more.

Tom told his brother that he was trying to get together the means for George to get out of the area, and possibly escape to Mexico. He just needed a little more time to finish a few last details and then George's life would be much better.

Once, Mexico would have been the preferred place to run to, but now, with the Mendoza Mob surely after George, he could no longer be certain Mexico was his best choice. He talked to his brother about Cuba, or Guatemala, or other Central American countries where he could live life off the grid and avoid being found. Tom understood, and was sympathetic toward George's plight, but he was not going to expose everyone just because his younger brother was getting 'antsy'. Tom told his brother to enjoy his freedom, however measured it is, and sit tight indoors. And be safe. George decided to explore the limited cable TV offerings, again, and see what he could find that is new. He also needed to make himself a sandwich and a cup of coffee.

Tom worried about his brother, George, and how long he could manage himself and his feeling of confinement. Tom worried, but right now, he was much more worried about his baby sister and her medical condition. He thought that he would call the hospital and see how much information he could garner from that phone call; otherwise, he would have to be a "hired-grandfather-clock-mechanic-who-heard-that-his-client-was-in-an-auto-accident" person and see if that got him anything additional.

Tom's best vendor representative, a classy Nicaraguan jewel salesman named Ernesto Siguenya, had once told Tom about his cousin's business of smuggling people into his country who were "somewhat being looked for." That term was something that Tom never asked for further explanation of, but just filed away in his memory. Now could be a good time to quiz Ernesto for further explanation, and possible use, of his cousin's services. Time will tell. The good thing about George, or any one of them, going to Nicaragua, is that even though Nicaragua has signed an extradition treaty with the United States, they are notorious for not extraditing criminals. If the criminal has lived a peaceful, contributing life in their country, not committed any crimes in their country, and has gone to mass and confession in church on a fairly regular basis, they will not assist in that person's extradition to the U.S. Treaty, or no treaty. Tom has long thought that this could be a good, safe place for him to retire to, and possibly live off the grid.

After checking his calendar of appointments, Tom sent George a coded message as to where, and how, the two of them would meet. Tom needed to give George more money, and a new company credit card so he could continue to live at the Extended Stay America, and buy food for himself.

They decided to meet, once again, at the Long Wharf Pier Park and eat lunch off the nearby food trucks. The day was cooler than normal, with low clouds hanging around throughout the day. After paying for their lunches, the two brothers walked over to a nearby picnic table to eat and talk. For George, this is a real treat! Talking face-to-face with a real person, and being outside where he can watch the seagulls and other birds fly up and down. Even an occasional drop of water from the mist in the air did not seem to bother George; he was enjoying being outside.

Tom explained to his brother what he was looking into, as it regards Nicaragua and George. Tom talked about the history of the country not enforcing their treaty with various countries, and especially the United States. George listened intently and asked many questions; most of the questions Tom could not answer yet, not until after he met with Ernesto.

They talked for quite a long while even after the light mist began to turn into light rainfall. They seemed to have a lot to catch up on, but George's attention was suddenly diverted from what Tom was saying over to the parking lot area. He watched the arrival of two older Chevrolet vans pull into the lot and begin to unload several Hispanic-looking men. All of the men seemed very determined to not want to look in the direction of the two men having lunch and talking. George began to survey the area to his left, and again to his right knowing that both his car, and Tom's car, were parked back beyond the group of men.

George told Tom what he was seeing over at the parking lot and how the two groups of men were beginning to fan out to George's left and right and that both of their cars were parked behind the two groups. George told Tom that he 'was packin' and would not hesitate to pull it out and take out a few of them, if necessary. Tom told his brother to keep it hidden and wait to see what was going to happen. "Too late," said George, "it's already under the table and ready for use." Again, Tom told his brother to be patient and wait. They didn't know what was about to happen, but George was not going to lay down and give these 'hombres' a chance to tear his body parts off and beat him to death with them. George watched the men split into two groups and then watched each group move in opposite directions, as though they were about to encircle the two men.

George told Tom that he had moved his gun close to his belt buckle and was waiting for one of the 'hombres' to make a move toward them. George told Tom that when the first shot was fired, Tom should bolt toward the water and dive in; that being cold and wet would feel better than being dead.

Tom agreed with his brother, but said that even the best, and fastest, swimmer was not going to out-distance a speeding bullet. George smiled and started to raise his right arm as the two groups of men continued to slowly move closer, stopping a the big open grass area about thirty yards from where they sat. George was just inches away from exposing his gun when the groups stopped, and he thought to himself about which man he would have to shoot first.

Suddenly, as the gentle rainfall began to increase and become less gentle, the two groups of men started tossing a football back-and-forth from group to group. One of the 'hombres' yelled over to Tom and George asking if they wanted to join in a friendly game of mud football. George yelled back his thanks, as he hid his gun inside his jacket better, saying that they both were recovering from hip replacements and could not run well. The man laughed and said 'okay' as he threw a perfect spiral down the field to another man.

Tom decided that the rain was now too heavy to continue sitting outside, so they had better be getting back to warmer, drier environments. But, Tom thought, they would end this by walking down the water's edge toward Long Wharf Pier and then over to where their cars are parked. Tom told his brother what his thinking is, and George replied "remember to limp, slightly. We've both had our hips replaced." Tom laughed, and said he would limp.

As the two brothers rose and started limping their way southwest along the waters edge toward 'Food Truck Paradise', they saw a police car making its' way onto Long Wharf Drive and passing under the turnpike above. The two men decided to just continue walking along talking to each other as if they were simply out for a nice stroll on a non-rainy day. They weren't, of course, but as the patrol car slowed slightly, Tom waved at the two officers inside, and continued talking to George.

The police car continued past the two brothers, stopping next to the parked food trucks. One officer jumped out and went to a truck to place his order for lunch, paying close inspection to the men playing touch football in the pouring rain.

After placing his food order, he gave a slight signal to his partner waiting in the patrol car. With that, his partner pulled the patrol car into a parking space, locked everything and came to the food truck as if to order his lunch. One officer talked to the cook in the food truck while the other officer watched the men running around in the mud, slipping and sliding with almost every step.

While watching, the officer talked to his dispatcher on his radio about what they were watching. Several minutes of conversation went by before the officer silenced his speaker and turned to look at his partner. Something in the way one officer looked at the other told the cook that he better hurry the cooking of the food along.

Tom and his brother had limped far enough away from the activity to be able to cross Long Wharf Drive and head for the parking lot and their cars. George continued to hide his gun inside his coat, but began to worry that with more and more rain falling on him, that his gun might slip out and fall onto the ground. Just as they reached their parked cars, Tom saw another police car slowly coming south on Long Wharf Drive toward them. Tom turned to see another police car parked at the southern end of the drive as it turned to go under the turnpike, and, still, another police car heading south on Long Wharf Drive toward the food trucks. Tom knew this was too many police cars for something simple; this was going to involve police action, and he didn't want it to involve he or George. He quickly told George what he saw and suggested they get in their cars and leave.

George agreed and unlocked his car doors to get inside. Just as Tom opened his car door to do the same, someone on a very loud bullhorn was shouting orders to "drop on the ground, with your arms folded behind your backs." Tom knew the sound of a police officer on a bullhorn, and he knew it would lead to a lot of questions for him and for George if they did not leave immediately. He motioned to George to leave just as the first gunshot rang out. Instinctively, he laid down on his front seat as several more shots rang out. Tom saw the tail lights of his brother's car move away and gradually go out of sight. He raised his head up to look out his windshield to confirm that it was George's car that had driven off just as a bullet smashed through the driver's side, rear window shattering glass and throwing it in every possible direction. With that Tom threw his body back down onto the front seat, ever thankful that he had driven his old car with the bench-type front seat. He knew he would have been in a world of hurt if he had driven his newer car with the bucket-type seats.

Gunshots continued for a several more minutes before Tom realized that the silence he was hearing was, hopefully, the end of the conflict. He stayed laying flat on his front seat for another couple minutes until, again, he heard the voice on the bullhorn saying "remain on the ground. Do not move, do not raise your head, put your hands out above your head with your fingers spread apart." The message was repeated by someone in Spanish before the original voice spoke again. "The people in the parked autos, roll down your windows and show your hands and arms out through the open windows. Do this now!"

With that, Tom rolled down his car window, sat up, and put his hands and arms out the window into the cold rain. He looked around expecting to see some of the policemen laying in pools of blood, but a few uniformed officers were busy handcuffing a couple muddy football players. Just then he saw what appeared to be two dead bodies laying in the parking lot area; one where George's car had been parked, and the second one about six feet away from Tom's driver's door.

Just then a uniformed officer came near Tom's car and asked him to slowly, with his left hand, reach for the outside door handle, open his driver side door and step out of the car. Tom complied and stepped into the falling rain with both arms raised above his head. Another officer came over and placed Tom's arms behind his back and placed both into handcuffs. While all this was going on Tom noticed that, of the ten or twelve men who had been playing football in the rain, only two were sitting upright with their arms cuffed behind their backs. The one, rather large and portly fellow, was the one who had thrown the long perfect spiral downfield; the pass that Tom stood admiring for a couple seconds. Tom noticed a distinctive large star tattoo on his neck. A large star similar to the type worn by the Dallas Cowboys football team, except this star has a large serpent going through the middle of the star to the back, and then coming back to the front of the star with a typical snake-with-fangs-showing finish. Not a tattoo that Tom would have chosen, had Tom decided to have a tattoo done on his neck. The others football players were laying in pools of rain and mud, or had plastic tarps placed over their lifeless bodies. Tom also noticed that all, but one, of the food trucks had left the area as more police cars were arriving with lights and sirens going. Along with additional police cars, two ambulances and a coroner's van arrived.

Having his arms cuffed securely, an office escorted Tom across the street to the remaining food truck where the medical techs from one ambulance were attending to the food truck's cook who laid motionless on the floor of the truck.

Tom realized that someone was asking him questions, and snapped his focus from the cook to the police officer in front of him. "Do you understand your rights, sir?" asked the officer. Tom tried clearing his throat several times before answering "I'm sorry. I did not hear what was being told to me." The officer smiled and read Tom's Miranda Rights to him once more before asking Tom, again, if he understood his legal rights. This time Tom said he did and asked if one of the cuffs could be loosened just slightly to allow blood flow through his hand and arm. The office checked Tom's cuffs and complied with Tom's request.

Five minutes later, an officer with Sargent's bars on his uniform approached Tom and asked him if he was hurt in any way. Tom said that he was not and asked what was going on here. The officer did not answer, instead asking Tom why he was here in the rain with a lot of other men. Tom told him that he had met a fellow here about two hours ago because the man had worked for Tom once, moved out of the area, had moved back and wanted to know if Tom had any jobs he could be hired for. The officer asked Tom what kind of business he was in. Tom replied that he owned several companies dealing in clocks, jewelry, real estate and an Ace Hardware store. The officer stopped writing down his notes and asked Tom what clock store he owned. When Tom answered, the officer smiled and said that his wife had taken an old family heirloom mantle clock there to have it fixed and a great job was done. The clock was still working perfectly. Tom told the office to thank his wife for the business and to bring it in every few years for maintenance.

The officer asked for Tom's name, home address, and home phone number and if Tom had identification on him to confirm any of this information. Just then, the coroner came over to the police Sargent and saw Tom in handcuffs. Recognizing Tom, the coroner asked how Tom was doing.

Realizing that the coroner recognized him, the Sargent started asking more, and more questions before becoming convinced that Tom was just a man who was in the wrong place at the wrong time.

The police Sargent removed Tom's handcuffs and asked to see Tom's driver's license for verification of his address. He then asked Tom for the name of the man that he had been with. Fortunately, Tom remembered the name of a stock clerk who once worked in his Ace hardware store, had moved away, and so he gave the officer that fellow's name. The Sargent jotted all this information down in his notebook before apologizing to Tom for what he had been put through. Tom said he understood that the officers only did what was necessary for everyone's security, and asked what prompted this level of police action.

The Sargent said that he could not discuss any particulars, but only say that the department had been shadowing this family gang for some time due to 'suspected' drug dealings. Tom simply wiped rain off his face and raised his eyebrows at the Sargent's remarks.

"Wow," said Tom, "I didn't think we had that sort of problem here in New Haven; or, in Connecticut for that matter." The Sargent said he wished that were the case, but it has become a problem everywhere. With that he apologized, again, and said that Tom was free to leave when he wanted. Before returning to his car, Tom asked the coroner how the food truck cook was doing since Tom really enjoyed the sandwiches he created. The coroner suggested that Tom find another food truck, as the cook had taken two bullets from the guys on the ground and didn't survive. Tom said how sorry he was, thanked the coroner for coming to his aid with the police officer, and walked back to the parking lot to get his car and leave.

Soaked to the bone, Tom couldn't wait to get home and put on some dry, clean clothes and have a hot cup of coffee. First, though, he had to send George a message and make certain that he made it back to his room in New London okay.

Message received okay. George was home okay. No problem.

Tom couldn't wait to tell George about all the fun he missed.

CHAPTER 9

The story in the morning paper simply told about the police responding to some men fighting after a football game in the park area of Long Wharf Pier last night. It went on to say that someone pulled a gun, discharged two rounds which struck the owner of "Tico's Tacos and Gourmet Sandwiches" food truck parked nearby. Two men were arrested at the scene and are being held in the New Haven jail pending the outcome of the police investigation into the incident.

Dr. Walker read the article in his morning paper and thought nothing about it, except that he thought it very unusual for someone to fire a gun in this city; especially, because of a football game. The shooter's team must have lost badly, he thought.

Tom Kitchen read the same story as he sat in the waiting room at the hospital where his sister laid close to death, and knew that there were many more facts behind the story than were being published. Tom thought about calling his friend, an assistant editor at the paper, but thought that would lead to too many questions which either could not be answered, or Tom would not want to have to answer. He thought about how close George and he had come to possibly being shot to death by one of these guys. He wondered how they had tracked George down and how they knew exactly where the two of them would be likely to meet. He remembered the long, cold stare without any trace of feelings that he got from the fellow with the unusual neck tattoo and how it would always send chills up and down his spine. He began to think that it could be time for George to head for parts unknown; traveling far and traveling soon. He decided to let the story play out and see what happened going forward. He turned to check on his favorite sports teams as a doctor walked up to him asking if he was the person asking about Sally Hamilton. Tom acknowledged that he is and began to explain that Mrs. Hamilton is a customer of his and he went to her home to do routine, scheduled, maintenance on her grandfather clock and heard about her auto accident. The young doctor apologized for not being able to give Tom all the details of her condition, but because he is not a close blood relative, hospital policy forbids him from giving out a detailed condition report. Tom said he understood, and thanked the doctor before turning to leave.

Tom had only taken a couple steps when another voice asked him to wait a minute. He turned to see another doctor standing talking to the young doctor that Tom had just talked to. The two doctors continued talking for another few seconds before the second doctor, whose sparkling white coat had the name Dr. Chambers embroidered on it, walked toward Tom.

"Hi, I am Dr. Chambers, Sally Hamilton's primary doctor and I have been told you are inquiring about her condition."

"I am," Tom answered. "Mrs. Hamilton is a very good client of mine, I happened to have business here, so I thought I would inquire about how she is doing. The other doctor explained to me the hospital policy for non-blood relatives, or friends, so I was about to leave."

Dr. Chambers smiled at Tom before saying "wow. Mrs. Hamilton must be a REALLY good client for someone to go out of their way to get an update on their condition. I'm sorry that we cannot say any more than she is in intensive care, and in critical condition, but if she gains consciousness, I will tell her you were inquiring about her. Who can I say stopped by?"

Just as Tom was about to give the doctor his name and the name of his hardware business, Johnny Hamilton walked around the corner of the hallway and made eye contact with Tom.

"Well, hello, Tom. What brings you here? On Business?" asked Johnny. Before Tom could answer, Dr. Chambers jumped into the conversation when he asked Johnny if he know this man, or not. "Yes, I do, doctor. Why?"

"He was asking about your wife's condition and we had to explain to him that hospital policy for non-blood relatives, or friends, is to not give out details concerning a patients' condition. Now, if you want to give him more details, that's quite all right. It's just that we cannot."

Johnny asked Tom if he had a couple minutes so that he could buy him a cup of coffee and fill him in on Sally. Tom looked at his watch knowing that he needed to get messages to George, but he also needed to know more about his little sister.

"If it is a quick cup," Tom answered, "I have the time. Can we get something out of a machine, or do we venture down to the cafeteria?" The two men went off to the hospital cafeteria to talk and have coffee.

The hospital cafeteria is a very sterile, bland appearing, strictly utilitarian room used mostly by visitors. Doctors and nurses, for the most part, prefer to get their own beverages, or food, elsewhere, or to buy food here and take it elsewhere to be consumed. A stark contrast can be made between this cafeteria and the cafeteria in the newer children's wing. Bright colors cover all the walls with 3-D cutouts of today's most popular super heroes or animals all around the brightly colored tables and chairs. Lines flow better, and the food and beverages just seem to taste better than in the 'old' hospital cafeteria.

It was only about fifteen minutes later that Tom Kitchen was thanking Johnny for the information updating Sally's condition and how the accident had happened. Johnny was so impressed by the 'story' that Tom had given him about coming to do regular maintenance on their grandfather clock and then hearing from a customer about Sally's accident, that Johnny never thought about the WHY of Tom's interest in Sally. So Johnny was glad to fill Tom in on just about everything before shaking hands and going their separate ways.

Tom's coded message to George was short and to the point, but brought no response from George. As Tom pulled his truck out of the hospital parking lot, he noticed three police cars being emptied of uniform officers. The police seem to fan out and go in three different directions. "Very strange behavior," Tom thought to himself. "Strange that so many uniformed officers would come to the hospital at the same time, unless they are in pursuit of someone." Tom drove about five blocks from the hospital before pulling into a parking lot and sending George another coded message. This time he would wait and see if he got a reply, or not.

Half an hour later Tom had not received a response from George and was beginning to fear the worse. He thought about the possibility that the police had located George's hotel and arrested him. He thought about the scarier possibility that the Mendoza Mob had caught up with George and had him in their custody. Either way, George was not answering any of Tom's messages and this worried him immensely.

Tom drove on to the Ace Hardware store to check with his newly-appointed manager on how the day's business was going and then on to the clock and jewelry stores. Tom was less concerned about his businesses right now than he was about his brother George's silence, but needed to keep his routine up. He tried one more coded message to George before leaving the jewelry store and heading back to the hardware store.

Tom was almost back to his hardware store when he got a coded message from George. Tom quickly pulled over and parked his truck, replied to his brother's message, and waited again. This time it was only a minute before Tom received a phone call from George telling him that he was concerned after the 'event' at Long Wharf Park and that he thought it would be better to relocate himself. Tom agreed, only to find out that George was now residing at the Hawthorn Suites on Main street in Meriden. Tom asked why there, and got a "why not?" reply from George. It made as much sense to Tom as anything was making right now.

Tom continued talking to his brother, but was becoming more and more concerned about a car that he had seen earlier that was now parked about a half block behind him. The car was rather flashy for Bridgeport with all of its' exposed chrome parts plated with gold, the exterior paint was a bright metallic red, and it has rather large "spinner" type wheels which made it rise above its' normal height. Tom could tell that there were men inside the car but was not able to tell how many. As he listened to George, Tom tried hard to remember where he had seen this car before. It is very distinctive, and with everything that has gone on lately, having this type car with several men sitting inside was making Tom nervous.

Tom told George to hold on the phone for a minute as he was going to move his car to another location. With that, Tom pulled out of the parking space and drove down the street for several blocks. He made multiple right hand turns to see if the car stayed behind him, or not; it did. When Tom next pulled over and parked, the other car did the same. Now he was getting nervous, again, and told George it was time for plan "B." George had the urge to start asking the three dozen questions he was thinking of, but decided that Tom knew best.

Their phone conversation ended abruptly and George started throwing some things into his duffle bag. Tom went on to the parking lot at the hardware store and parked his truck in a 'reserved' parking space. This time the flashy red car was not in sight. Tom didn't know what worried him more: seeing the car full of men following him everywhere, or NOT seeing the car full of men anywhere.

Tom went into his hardware store and directly into his office. He made several phone calls, went over the day's receipts with his manager, gave him a list of items that Tom would need for "a project", and told his manager that he had to leave for a while and would be in contact with him soon. With that, Tom left the hardware store and got into his 4-wheel drive Jeep parked in another 'reserved' space and sped out of the lot.

The more Dr. Walker did around the clinic, the less time Dr. Greybar spent at the clinic. In a very short time almost every patient of Dr. Greybar's had become a new patient of Dr. Walker. Dr. Greybar had expected this to happen within this period of time, if he found the right partner to bring into the clinic, and he was more than glad that he had chosen Dr. Gerald Walker.

Dr. Walker was just finishing with physical exams for three local high school boys who had signed up for school football and had to get physicals and approval from their doctor before getting any uniforms. Dr. Walker signed their approval letters, and reminded one of the boys that he had to use an ointment the doctor had given him for toe fungus, or suffer the consequences. As he was saying goodbye to the boys and wishing them good luck in this years' football schedule, two very big men in dark suits and dark sunglasses came through the office door.

One man asked for Gerald Walker, by name, while he handed the receptionist his business card. She looked at the card while glancing over toward Dr. Walker who stood nearby wondering why these two men looked vaguely familiar. Finally the receptionist asked Dr. Walker if he could see these men. After looking at the business card and seeing that one man is Darren Miller of the FBI, Dr. Walker asked the two men to follow him into his office.

"To what do I owe the pleasure of this visit?" asked Dr. Walker as he sat in his office chair. "Does the FBI need to have physical exams performed?"

"Thanks for the offer, doctor, but we are here on official business." Answered Darren Miller. "This gentleman is special agent Devon Miller of the NSA. He is my brother, but more importantly, he is working on the same case as I am, only from a national security standpoint." Devon Miller gave the doctor one of his cards as they shook hands with each other. Darren Miller asked Dr. Walker if he had a patient with the name of Keeper, or Kiefer, or if he knew anyone with those last names. Dr. Walker said he did not. Then Darren Miller showed the doctor a photo of Guido Kiefer taken at a wedding reception. Dr. Walker studied the photo for a couple minutes before saying "yes, I have seen this man before, but I do not know him. He was involved in my sister Stephanie's wedding some time ago, but I never remember seeing him after that."

Darren Miller asked if Dr. Walker's sister would know more about him, to which the doctor answered that this man was one of his brother-in-law, Derek's groomsmen, not a friend of his sister Stephanie.

Dr. Walker asked what all of this was in regards to, this Kiefer fellow, and such. Agent Miller told the doctor that it is an ongoing Federal investigation and that they are not able to discuss any of the details. Devon Miller told the doctor that both state and federal agencies had interests in talking to this Kiefer fellow in regards to, still, another person.

After a few more questions about the doctor's family, and his sister's wedding, the two agents thanked Dr. Walker for his time and cooperation, and asked him to contact either of them if he remembered anything new or came into contact with the Kiefer fellow. Dr. Walker assured them that he would, and walked with them to the front door just as more high school football team members showed up for their physicals. He gave instructions to the group of 'want-a-be' athletes as to which exam room to go into and how far down they had to strip and watched the small group walk off down the hallway.

It was then that a picture popped into Dr. Walker's head; a picture of a near-death, bloodied body man with two bullets in his body laying on the clinic's operating table. Dr. Walker opened the front door to his clinic and ran outside to see how far the two agents had gone. Fortunately, Agent Darren Miller had to stop about one hundred feet away from the clinic to take a phone call. Dr. Walker called out to the two agents, waved at them, and proceeded to walk forward toward them saying "I just had a visual flashback."

Agent Darren Miller ended his phone call and started

walking back toward the doctor saying "I'm sorry, you had a what?"

When the men got within a few feet of each other, Dr. Walker repeated "I just had a visual flashback. I have seen that man you are looking for recently. In fact, Dr. Greybar and I had him in our OR removing two bullets from his chest before turning him over to the New Haven Police. Can I see your picture again?"

Agent Darren Miller fished through his folder of documents, found a picture of Kiefer, and showed it to Dr. Walker. The doctor studied it few several seconds before looking at Agent Darren and confirming that this is, in fact, the man that he and Dr. Greybar had operated on and removed two bullets from. Dr. Walker apologized to the two agents saying that when he saw this fellow he was a mess of blood, scratches, bruises, and near death. Being near death, his skin coloring was so pale and different that he did not see his patient as being the fellow in the color photo. He also said that the photo was somewhat blurry and out of focus when compared to his mental picture of the man laying on the OR table. The agents understood and began to ask many additional questions as Amanda came out the front door of the clinic calling for Dr. Walker.

Dr. Walker asked the two agents if they could come back in about an hour and he would have more time to answer whatever questions they still had, as he had to complete the physicals for the young men waiting for him so that they could return to school. Agent Darren said that they would get a cup of coffee at the nearby Starbuck's and come back.

Tom was beyond nervous at what was going on; things that HE could not control and did not know the full extent of. He moved his Jeep quickly onto northbound I-91 hoping that not taking I-95 to Boston would fool anyone that might want to follow him or pick them up along the way. He planned everything out to the 'n-th' possible degree and hoped, again, he was right. He would continue north to Hartford where he would take I-84 into Massachusetts and eventually have it turn into I-90 which would take him directly into Boston. With every passing mile, Tom felt better and better about his choice of routes. He hoped that George stuck to the "plan B" plan and took the routes the plan called for; anything else, could be big problems for his brother.

Before leaving, Tom had contacted the hospital to check on the condition of his little sister, Sally. He was not able to find out anything new until he talked to the head nurse, and she had told Tom that Sally's husband was about to make a decision as to whether, or not, Sally would be kept alive by machines, or allowed to fight for her life herself, naturally. This news hit Tom very hard as he always felt like he was his little sister's protector, even though no one knew they were related. He tried to remember all the times that he had been unable to defend her from some bully, or protect her from a bad situation throughout her life. Those memories bothered Tom tremendously. Tremendously. He knew that most of what had happened was for her benefit; growing up without the daily contact of her siblings was her protection from what all four of the children knew. Knew about that horrible night so long ago.

Tom seemed to be lost in many, many thoughts and memories, and did not notice the dark brown car that seemed to be shadowing him from two hundred yards back in traffic. He barely even noticed the upcoming city limits of Hartford and reminded himself that there would be plenty of time for reminiscing about past events and times after his task was done.

Tom made the transition from I-91 onto I-84 without any problems, but did finally notice the dark brown car with the very distinctive 'spinner-type' wheels on it as it made the same north-to-east transition onto I-84. Again, Tom began to feel uncomfortable and decided to slow down a little and let the car pass him. As Tom slowed, the dark brown car slowed. When Tom sped up substantially, so did the dark brown car. As Tom changed lanes on the interstate, the dark brown car changed lanes; the dark brown car mirrored everything that Tom would do in his Jeep.

Tom was so focused on the dark brown car that he did

not see the flashy red car with the gold plated chrome and "spinner" type wheels come onto the interstate at a rapid rate of speed, and nestled into a spot about four car lengths ahead of Tom's Jeep. Tom continued to change speeds and lanes, and the dark brown car continued to do exactly the same thing.

It was during one of Tom's lane changing maneuvers that he noticed the flashy red car with the gold plated chrome moving along in a spot about three car lengths ahead of him. Now, this is a car he recognizes, including the four or five men inside. Okay, he thought, what do you do now, smarty? Do you try to out run cars that could have high power engines under their hoods? Or, do you try to 'out fox' them? Choice number one was dismissed by Tom immediately; his four-wheel Jeep was not made for racing, of that he was certain.

Tom continued thinking about his situation as he saw multiple large highway signs warning of construction coming ahead. "Construction Zone Ahead" he thought. As he watched the flashy red car slow down and get within two car lengths of Tom's Jeep, he also studied the areas off the roadway. Tom did not have a plan in mind, largely because he did not have any idea what the men in the two cars were planning. He knew he would have to make a stop soon for gas or he would be running out on the interstate and would probably have both car loads of men keeping him company.

Tom saw a roadside sign advertising a 'Tolland Citgo' service station on Merrow Road, which he knew was the next off ramp. Unsure about the area, and unsure about how exposed he might be when getting gas at the Citgo station, Tom was reluctant to try this station. As he got closer to the off ramp, Tom saw more signs advertising diners, a Dunkin Donut shop and several other businesses and began to feel better about there being other people around. He didn't know what the men in the two fancy cars wanted him for, but he felt that they would not try anything with people around. He hoped he was right.

Tom eased his Jeep off the Interstate and into the Citgo gas station and was glad to see lots of people around the area; both at the Citgo, and adjacent U-haul rental business. Tom began filling the thirsty Jeep gas tank and was feeling better about his decision when he felt something hard and cold being pressed into his right kidney area of his back.

"Do not turn around" a soft spoken Latin voice said. "Do not think, for a moment, that I will not kill you right here, right now. Now, stop filling the tank, hand me your car keys, and slowly, very slowly move backwards toward me. Be very careful, bro, as this fuckin' gun has a very nervous trigger on it."

Tom thought about what the man had told him and he knew that if he went with this guy, he would end up dead somewhere out in a field. "This is a cash purchase, so I have to go pay the cashier for the gas I pumped," Tom told the unseen man.

"We will pay for the gas, you do as I say as my nervous trigger is beginning to shake. MOVE!" The man gave no indication of being patient or caring anything about Tom's situation other than what he told Tom to do. Just as Tom began to reach into his pants pocket to get his car keys, two young men came up to them from behind asking if Tom was ever going to finish at this pump and move on so someone else could use it. The Latin man behind Tom told the two guys to get lost that they were not finished filling his tank and paying. As the man with the gun turned to look at the other two men Tom went pushing backwards with as much force as he could. As he did this, the man's gun went off sending a bullet grazing Tom's right side slightly, and startled everyone around.

Tom had used enough force going backwards to shove the Latin man into the two younger men and sending all three sprawling onto the ground. Tom, on the other hand, kept his balance, opened the driver's door to his Jeep, started the engine and was exiting the gas station onto Merrow Road. As he pulled away from the pump he noticed both fancy cars parked nearby; one at the entrance to the gas station, and the fancy red car across the road near the on ramp to the interstate. Tom was heading in the opposite direction and did not have a clear idea as to where he should go.

Tom saw that he had been able to fill the gas tank above the half way point, so he knew he had enough gas to get up the road towards Boston; he just didn't know exactly what direction to take now. He followed Merrow Road through the little community of Tolland and had driven almost five minutes before sensing a severe pain in his right side. He put his hand there and felt the warm liquid which he knew was blood. He knew he needed to look at his injury but also knew that he did not have time right now to attend to anything other than escape.

Tom knew that the two car loads of men were behind him somewhere and that they would easily catch him on this road. Without hesitation, Tom made a rapid left turn onto Walbridge Hill Road and watched in his rear view mirror to see if any cars were following him. He drove on for about ten minutes before making another left turn and then a right turn onto S. River Road. After a couple minutes more he entered the town of Willington and state highway 32. Tom remembered that highway 32 was the next off ramp from the interstate, so he felt confident that if he headed north on highway 32, he would join up with the interstate again.

Therein could be the problem for Tom: getting back onto Interstate 84 where the two fancy cars would be looking for him. Since the brother's 'plan B' called for them to meet again outside of Boston, it was not mandatory for Tom to get there via I-84. What was quickly becoming mandatory for Tom to handle was his bleeding and injured right side. Fortunately, when he gave his hardware store manager a list of needed items for this trip, a large first aid kit was one of the items listed. While Tom was not anxious to be 'doctoring' himself, he knew he had to tend to his wound in order to be moving forward toward Boston and the rendezvous with his brother.

Though it hurt like a 'son-of-a-gun', Tom cleaned up his wound and put a large dressing on it. Fortunately for him the bullet only grazed him and did not go deeply into his side. He then grabbed a clean shirt to put on before moving his Jeep out of the wooded clearing where he had parked off of the main road.

Tom stopped at the Willington Fire Department headquarters knowing that they would have a map of this area. He was right. A very obliging off-duty fireman showed Tom the large, detailed, map of the area that hung on the wall in the back of the firehouse. The fireman asked Tom a lot of questions about where he was heading to, what direction he had come from, and others questions that had Tom feeling a little uncomfortable. Tom quickly found that state route 44 east would take him, in an indirect way, to Providence, Rhode Island where he could connect to I-95 north to Boston. He doubted that whoever the men are in the two fancy cars, they would not be looking for him in

Rhode Island, nor on I-95. Tom made several notes mapping out the unusual, indirect route that he will be taking as the fireman continued to ask his questions. Tom smiled as he finished his notes, and thanked the young fireman very much for his help.

Before Tom left on his carefully mapped out route, he had to go the opposite way on highway 32 to the closest gas station to finish filling up the tank of his Jeep. This accomplished, Tom headed east on state route 74 until he reached highway 44, which he would take all the way to Providence.

CHAPTER 10

Gerald Walker had taken many, many courses during his medical studies which dealt with death and how to handle both the medical aspect of it, as well as the psychological aspect. Taken many courses dealing with death, but when it is the death of someone within your family, someone whom your wife and children are very close to, all the courses and studies do not begin to adequately instruct a person how to make death painless.

Gerald was thinking about death as he guided the family van into the long driveway of Stephanie and Derek's Victorian mansion. Thinking about death and not really paying attention to what his wife, Gerri was saying to him. She said something about a 'broom', or something about not having enough 'room.' Whatever it was, he was not going to admit to her that he was not paying full attention to what she was saying.

"Well, did you?" Gerri asked her husband. "Did you reserve us any rooms at a hotel? This is the third time I have asked you."

"Honestly, since I got the call that Sally had died, I have not thought much about hotel rooms. Sorry. I should have, but I didn't do it. Besides, Stephanie said there are enough spare bedrooms on the second floor to accommodate us as long as the boys sleep together, and the girls do the same. Let's see what is available at the Victorian before we search elsewhere." With that, Gerald Walker leaned back in the driver's seat, exhaled slowly and looked around the area. Even in the dark, the old Victorian mansion seemed to have a life of its' own; as if it were watching everyone and every move and waiting to pass judgement as to who stayed and who left. Funny, thought Gerald, he had not seen this aspect of the grand old Victorian when he had seen it in the light of day. At night, though, it looked completely different. Alive, but not full of life. Watching, but not wanting to see everything. And then there was that faint odor of rotting meat that Gerald was beginning to get a whiff of. As the moon slid out from behind a cluster of clouds, it framed the Victorian in a cold glow that made it look as though it were examining everyone in the van; the shadow that the house cast upon the doctor's family seemed almost surreal and welcoming. Welcoming, and yet in some ways, menacing. The grand old Victorian mansion, Keeper House, was telling Dr. Gerald Walker that it would choose the time and place to exert its' evil upon any one of them.

Again, his wife was talking to him and he was not hearing a single word she said. "Will you help me get the children out of the van and into the house?" Gerri asked her husband. "Of course I will," Gerald answered as he got out of the van and opened the side door. With the children all awake and walking on their own, Gerald grabbed a couple suitcases from the back of the van and walked up the steps of the old Victorian.

Stephanie and Derek were busy greeting Gerri and each of the children when Gerald walked through the front doorway. Sitting the suitcases down in the entryway, he exchanged hugs and handshakes with Stephanie and Derek. He added his "thanks" to that of Gerri for Stephanie and Derek opening up their house for his family to stay at while they all attended Sally's funeral. Derek offered to help Gerald get the remaining suitcases out of their van while Stephanie got Gerri and the children set up in their sleeping quarters; then it would be hot chocolate and cookies for the children, and wine and cheese and conversation for the adults.

She had to be half way through the second glass of cabernet before Gerri could being herself to ask Stephanie about the details of Sally's death. With Gerri and Sally being really good friends, Gerri felt as though she had a right to know more details about her friend's final days and weeks. Stephanie understood Gerri's desire to know how much her good friend had suffered, and told Gerri everything that she knew about Sally from the time of the collision until Sally's heart stopped. Doctor Gerald added the little bit of medical information that he knew and had gotten from the medical staff at the hospital where Sally was.

Somehow, knowing the facts about Sally's final weeks, and months, did not lessen the hurt that Gerri felt. But, right in the midst of all the conversing about Sally, Gerri asked how Johnny was doing. With that question, everyone stopped talking, and looked at each other with that look of 'not knowing' how to answer Gerri's question.

Finally, Derek inhaled deeply and said "he's doing fine now, but for a while he was not doing too well. He was on a sort of road trip driving around to various branches to check on matters, and was spending the night in Albany when he got the news about Sally's passing. The news must have hit Johnny so hard that he blacked out and had to be taken to the emergency room for treatment. After several hours, Johnny was taken back to the hotel and he drove home that same day. We both have talked to him, and to his sister Carla, and he seems to be handling it well. He is a man who went from having a wife, a daughter and two sons, to being alone. Alone in a home that has many, many ghosts and memories for him. It will take him a long time to climb the mountain that he has in front of him."

Everyone sat quietly and gently nodded their heads up and down in agreement. The silence seemed to last an hour, but it was only a couple minutes and was broken by Gerri's youngest son coming into the room saying that his brother was 'cheapin' in the game they were playing. Gerri smiled at him and asked him if he meant that his brother was "cheating" in the game. He nodded yes and everyone laughed and decided that it was time to put youngsters to bed. With that, all four adults got up and started off to gather up children and get them comfortably into their beds.

Later, after the children had been readied for bed and had fallen asleep, Gerald and Gerri Walker went for a long walk around the grounds of the Victorian, and down along the Saugatuck River. The evening was made for walking, hand-in-hand, talking about life and looking at the world alive in the light of a full moon. Gerald had asked Derek many questions about his yacht, how many lessons they had to take to become licensed to sail it, and how often they were able to get away on it. As they walked around Gerald got a full view of the ship tied up to their dock and thought that he, too, might enjoy owning something similar some day. Some day. He had a business partner to finish paying off what was owed for the medical clinic, and then there is the matter of four little people, now sound asleep in the Victorian, that would need to be put through school, with possible graduate studies. Dr. Gerald Walker's ship has already sailed, he thought.

The following day was busy visiting with friends and family that had come into town for Sally's services. The mood among everyone was somber and dark, and was made even more sullen by the approach of a rare long island sound hurricane which was making its' way up the eastern seaboard. All the weather people agreed that the 'cane' would certainly hit Connecticut, Rhode Island and parts of Massachusetts after it finished off the New Jersey and New York coastlines. It made traveling short distances just as difficult as traveling longer distances and no one was immune to problems that it created. The winds blew, and the rain came straight down at the same time that the rain came sideways. There seemed to be a wall of rain, after a wall of rain, which pounded everything and everyone.

Derek made certain that the "Stephanie's Joy" yacht was secured in its' slip before going back into the house to get ready for the services. He knew that this hurricane would cause some damage to buildings and to boats not properly secured in their moorings, but he did not want his to be one of them. He and Stephanie had learned from their friends at the yacht club how to handle securing a boat during a severe storm; and New England states were always having some type of severe storm during each year. The special air bags and equipment that Derek had installed in their slip had been very expensive, but he knew that if it saved their yacht, it would be well worth the cost.

Carla and Carl handled almost all the arrangements for Sally's services and burial, as they had also done for the children as they passed away. Both felt that they were becoming too expert in funeral arrangements, but were very glad to be able to lessen Johnny's burden in whatever way they could.

Although the hurricane had begun to weaken and had passed beyond Bridgeport before the services began, its' effects were still the reason that the mortuary was less than half full. Wind, heavy rain, and impaired visibility created travel conditions that only the bravest of people would challenge. As the service continued on, the storm intensified bringing increased winds, rain, and loud strong claps of thunder. It grew in strength to the point that the directors of the cemetery phoned Carla and advised against any possibility of a graveside service for the family. Even Father Carlon, the family's retired priest and friend, said that he had never seen a storm this bad in his 84 years.

Those who did not have to leave, or simply wanted to wait inside for a better time to brave the storm outside, enjoyed a luncheon in the large hall of the mortuary. The catered lunch was sponsored by Mr. & Mrs. Walker, who felt that people would want to relax and converse after a very emotionally draining funeral service. Many people saw the spread of food and beverages that the catering company has arranged and decided to wait out the storm and relax.

Father Carlon sat at a table with the Walkers, Johnny, and Carl and Carla, and kept the conversation light and moving. Being of Irish descent, the priest was able to inject timely, humorous Irish jokes and stories. He had been the priest that baptized all the Walker children, and married almost all of them except for Andrea and Andrew, and Johnny and Sally. So it was natural for Father Carlon to be curious about the funeral program listing Sally's name as 'Sally Ann Keeper Hamilton. Johnny thought for a moment before telling the priest that the story behind that answer would take much more time than they had left in the day. The priest told Johnny that he did not know how many more days God would allow him to enjoy, so he would like to know the story before too long. Johnny agreed to meet with Father Carlon soon at the church's rectory, and answer his questions about Sally.

As the storm began to dwindle, people said their 'good byes' to Johnny and members of the Walker family and left to go home. It was then that Johnny began to realize that this was final; that this was the last part of the last function of his last family member. It was now that he realized that he was alone, no longer one of five family members. No longer a father, nor a husband, simply one man. Alone.

Before he started to cry in front of the family members, Johnny got up from the table and went outside. Into the downpour of a passing storm cell he walked without a coat, without an umbrella, without concern for himself getting wet or cold. He simply had to walk away from the well wishes, and from the memories that were beginning to fill his head. He had to walk himself into a better mindset before trying to continue on with this day. As he walked, he saw his home, which now would be completely empty and cold without Sally and the children, and wondered to himself just how long he would continue to live there. A large, beautiful home which now had become much too large for one person had him thinking about the possibility of selling it and downsizing to a smaller townhouse, or condo. He told himself "if the Walkers can do it, then I certainly can, also."

Johnny was so caught up in his thoughts that he hardly noticed Carla's voice calling to him as she rushed after him in the rain. "You're going to drown out here without an umbrella or a coat," Carla told him. "You're already soaked to the bone and turning blue. You need to come back inside with me and get warm and dry."

Johnny looked at his sister standing next to him with drops of rain falling from the brim of her rain hat onto the tip of her nose and wondered why all this had happened. Why was he having to go through all this? First, the accident, which killed his oldest son and sent his wife and his other two children to the hospital. Then his daughter died. Then his five year old son died, and finally, his wife. "Why me?" he kept asking, knowing that he was not going to hear an answer in his ear. "What have I done to deserve any of this?" Johnny now felt very tired and emotionally drained. He began to feel the weight of everything pile up on his shoulders and the load was almost unbearable. He looked into his sister's eyes, drew upon all the strength he could muster, and showed her a faint smile as they started to walk back down the street toward the mortuary.

With everything that Johnny was now lacking, he knew he had family. Family that would help him, and support him.

He thought it a bit ironic that as he and Carla turned onto the sidewalk that leads to the front doors of the mortuary, a big ray of sunshine came out, the rain stopped, and for a brief moment the world seemed almost bearable.

After all the guest and friends had left the mortuary, the family checked on conditions at the cemetery and found out that a brief grave side ceremony could be held. It was Johnny who decided that he would like to finalize things with the grave side ceremony before leaving. The family understood and all got into their autos to travel the four miles to the cemetery and Sally's gravesite.

Already it had been a very long day for the family, but Stephanie and Derek wanted to give everyone the chance to wind down and relax by having a catered Italian dinner at their home. Pasta, salad, and lots of wine for the adults, and Italian sodas for the children, would possibly help to take away the aches from the day's events. Relaxing never seemed to hurt anyone's egos, and Stephanie knew that Johnny could really use some 'down time.'

Glass of wine in one hand, Johnny sat down in a huge over-stuffed wingback chair in the living room and fixated on the fire that was burning in the fireplace. Watching the flames dance up and down, he knew the world would someday return to normal; what ever 'normal' really is.

CHAPTER 11

Tom's decision to alter his route to Boston was a good decision. He was able to make the remainder of the trip without problems, made contact with George, and met with his contact Ernesto Siguenya to enlist his help in getting George out of the country safely. Tom and Ernesto met at the Los Amigos restaurant in the Chelsea district because Ernesto's brother-in-law is part owner and Ernesto knew they could get a quiet table in a corner where they could conduct their business. Ernesto, being of Nicaraguan ancestry, favored the Chelsea area of Boston because of its' heavily Latin population. He knew if he needed help at any time, he could get it there.

The food was very good, the Mexican beer very cold, and the talking with Ernesto very much to the point and fast. Ernesto will get Tom's brother a job as a deck hand on a Nicaraguan oil tanker and set him up with contacts when he lands in Managua. George will be set up in a hacienda of his choosing and given as much protection as he desires. All this, of course, will be provided for a tidy sum of U.S. Dollars which will be deposited by Tom in a Canadian Bank account known only by a number.

Tom liked the arrangements, and, after discussing every detail with George, made the first deposit of money into Ernesto's Canadian bank account. George went aboard the oil tanker while in port and spent three days learning every part of being a top-notch deck hand. George was able to fit right in with the rest of the deck hands and put his fluency in Spanish to good use.

The Nicaraguan oil tanker left port near Boston with one port-of-call at 'Refineria Isla' in Willemstad, on the island of Curacao. A regular stop by this ship to off-load cargo of a non-petroleum nature. George knew about the drop-off of cargo, but elected to pay attention to his job and nothing else that went on. The tanker also off-loaded some petroleum to make the stop look more legitimate to anyone who might investigate.

With his brother George safely out of the country, Tom returned to his daily routines of his businesses and sighed a great deal more. It had been several days since he had seen any of the numerous 'fancy' cars loaded with men. He didn't miss seeing them, but once again, felt there was a certain uneasiness about NOT seeing them. He found himself always looking over his shoulder, checking his car completely before getting into it, and constantly checking his surroundings for anything that Tom deemed 'out of place.'

With one sister dead, and one brother out of the country in hiding, Tom decided it was time to get in touch with his last remaining sibling: his younger sister Helen. He knew that by doing this, it could place her in jeopardy, but their plans had always been built around the four of them being able to pass the 'baton of life' along from one sibling to another. The 'baton of life' referred to a very unique key that Tom had been the keeper of for all his life. His sister Helen would have to become the keeper of all things of importance and meaning. Tom knew it was time to send her a coded message and wait for a response.

Tom's day-to-day business was keeping him busy and making him lots of money; money he was going to be sending to Ernesto Siguenya for George's safe keeping. Tom had mixed feeling about the amount of money he would have to spend for George's safety, but knew it was necessary, because in George's situation, there simply were not a lot of options available.

So Tom sent a coded message to his sister and waited for a coded response. The message was brief, and simple, and gave his sister a couple of options on how she would respond. Tom knew it would take a few days before he might get a response because of her lack of usage of the codes, and the fact that her code was a three step code which required much more time. As Tom thought about the message, and his sister, he was, once again, amazed at how complex, yet how simple, all these codes are that the four siblings have used for many, many years. Codes that Tom, and George, worked to set up years ago when they were but teenagers; codes that have kept them all in touch with one another despite distances, and other factors. With the codes, the boys also created scenarios that could possibly come up with each of them, and two or three different plans that could be used for each of the scenarios. But, enough of the self 'patting-on-the-back' thought Tom, there was plenty of work to be done before he would get a response back, and he had to check in on his jewelry store and see if he was making any money there.

As Tom walked out of the hardware store offices and down the stairs to the main floor, he saw his manager talking to a smartly-dressed young woman who was taking many notes of their conversation. Tom knew instantly that she was a reporter, but did not recognize her from any of the local TV stations. He decided that whomever she is, and whatever it is that she is seeking, he did not have time for her, or it. He ducked down a side aisle that would take him away from the reporter and eventually over to a side delivery door that he could use to go outside to his Jeep. As he turned a corner to head for the side door he heard his manager say "there he is! There's Tom Kitchen now." And with that, Tom's quick, unseen escape was thwarted.

Tom turned around to see the young woman, his store manager, and the woman's cameraman coming down the aisle toward him waving and smiling. Tom returned the smile but was wishing to himself that he had been a lot faster in getting to the parking lot.

Tom's manager introduced the reporter as Janice Wilkins, a reporter with CNN, and said that she was interested in getting background information on local successful businessmen.

Janice had a big smile on her face when she shook hands with Tom and said that she also was interested in Tom's feelings about the future for local, or small businessmen in the Connecticut coastal area. "Since you own diverse types of businesses, Mr. Kitchen, I wonder if I can get your opinions on a couple of questions that I've asked other business people from Stamford to Stonington."

Tom thought for a second and said "I would love to answer your questions and give my thoughts, but it would have to be another time. I'm already late for an appointment and can't reach the other party by phone. Can we make a date and follow up on this another day?" Tom asked. Janice Wilkins agreed to come back in two days and meet early morning before the activity level at the hardware store picked up. Tom thanked her, said he would look forward to seeing her in two days and rushed out the side door to the parking lot.

As Tom started his Jeep up and headed for the street, he stopped to check his cell phone. No coded response from his sister, so he headed onto the street and over to his jewelry store. Tom really did not have an appointment, he simply did not want to stand and talk to a TV reporter, especially a reporter from CNN. Tom suspected that she was looking for more than she divulged, and that gave him an uneasy feeling.

Tom arrived at the jewelry store and immediately went to work in the back room on a 'special' piece of jewelry for a special customer. He had fashioned a yellow gold necklace, ornate with jewels and numerous diamonds, to which he was now attaching an ornate gold, oddly shaped, key. Tom worked on this necklace for nearly three hours until he was satisfied that it was exactly as he wanted it. He then wrapped it with jeweler's cloths, placed it in a specially designed case which he carefully packed inside a box, before wrapping the whole thing in brown kraft paper for shipping. But Tom would not be shipping this piece of jewelry, he would hand deliver it, himself.

When finished, Tom talked to his manager about the day's business activity before leaving the store with his delivery.

Delivery done, Tom checked his cell phone once again for a coded response from his sister. No response. Tom was not going to over react, but it had been nearly five hours since he sent his message, and he expected, by now, that he would have some form of response. Tom thought about this for a minute and decided that he would move on to other business. A response from his sister was important, but so are other matters; matters that demand his immediate attention.

Dr. Walker was visiting a long time friend of his in the

hospital in Bridgeport when he heard that the Chief of Staff of the new children's hospital has been missing. Apparently Dr. Helen Eldon had left a meeting with staff and department heads four days ago, and had not been seen or heard from since. All attempts to contact her, and her husband, had failed.

Concern was rising also at New York University, where the husband of the Chief of Staff, Dr. Milton Eldon, PHD, is a professor of Ancient Greek Philosophy. Their concern is about the professor's disappearance some four days earlier, at the same time that his wife went missing. The professor was scheduled to meet with a group of doctoral candidates after a departmental meeting concluded, but did not. He was last seen going into a men's restroom on the same floor as his meeting was to be held, and has not been seen, nor heard from, since.

Dr. Walker had met the Chief of Staff at the dedication of the children's hospital, but did not know her or her husband well. People who did know her, said that this kind of action was very atypical for her and was certainly cause for alarm. The Bridgeport police were notified, as were the NYPD, and both departments have contacted the FBI for their assistance. This all seemed very strange to Dr. Walker and he hoped the situation would be resolved quickly.

When Dr. Walker finished visiting his friend, he phoned his wife, Gerri, who was driving down from New Haven, with their children so the entire family could go for a cruise with Derek and Stephanie on their yacht. The invitation had been extended, and the weekend cruise planned, when the family got together for Sally's funeral services. Gerri was very glad that the weather for this weekend was much better than that weekend; the storms had gone away and the sun was forecasted to be bright and warm. Most important to Gerri: the water is supposed to be smooth as glass. This one item pleased Gerri more than just about anything else as she did not consider herself a very good swimmer, and 'glassy-smooth' waters would put her mind at ease.

The doctor's children were beyond excited to be going out onto the ocean on "Uncle Derek's boat", and Gerri had a very difficult time getting them to quiet down enough for her to answer her husband's phone call. Gerri told her husband that she would pick him up in about ten minutes in front of the hospital and he could take over control of the excited bunch. Gerald agreed and let his wife concentrate on her driving.

As Gerald Walker stood outside in front of the hospital, he marveled at how nice the sun felt and how beautiful the blue sky seemed to be. No clouds, no wind, no storms coming into the area, he suddenly looked forward to a nice, relaxing weekend with Stephanie and Derek on the yacht. He always enjoyed sailing as a boy, and this would be his return to his childhood, and possibly a childhood dream;

that dream of owning, or piloting, a big boat.

As Gerald Walker enjoyed the sun beating down upon his face, a red Jeep pulled up to the curb in front of him and parked. Gerald was going to say something to the driver about parking in a 'Fire Lane', but the driver jumped out and ran into the hospital so quickly that he never got a chance to. As Gerald was pondering the situation, Gerri pulled their family van into a spot in front of the Jeep and gently tap the horn to get his attention. Gerald looked at the van loaded with his family and decided to leave the Jeep driver alone; let someone else play parking cop.

Gerald climbed into the van and settled in for the short ride down to Bridgeport and Keeper House where Stephanie and Derek lived. Gerald spent the time talking with his two older children about their days at school, their sport teams, and with his wife, Gerri, about the hectic schedule they all seemed to be keeping up with.

As Gerri pulled the van onto the long driveway at Keeper House, Gerald saw Stephanie waving at them from the back of the boat. He pointed out Stephanie's motioning to them so that Gerri could move the van back to the rear of the property and park.

Their kids were so keyed up and excited that they hardly waited for the van's engine to stop before unbuckling their seatbelts and bolting out of the van. They ran around the van chasing each other before running full speed toward the yacht. Stephanie yelled out to the kids for everyone to "STOP!! Stop where you are and freeze!"

Stephanie stood very tall and looked imposing with her nautical clothes and hat on. Whether it was the way she looked, or her strong, commanding voice that she used to yell at the kids, it got their immediate attention. All of them stopped in their tracks and stood completely still like little toy soldiers.

"Your Uncle Derek is the Captain of this boat!" Stephanie told the children. "Do you all understand that? He is the person that we all take orders from, and his decision is final. In order to get ONTO the boat you must be in a single file to get your life jacket. Your life jacket must be worn at ALL times while on the boat. You cannot touch or play with anything, because doing so could make things very dangerous for all of us!" With that, Stephanie gave Gerri and Gerald a wink of her eye and came down off the yacht with an armload of bright orange life jackets.

Either Stephanie 'put the fear' into the children, or they became so fascinated with everything that was happening on the yacht, that they became perfect onboard guests. They watched their Uncle Derek as he navigated out of the boat slip and piloted the boat onto the Saugatuck River, and down into the Long Island Sound. They asked questions about things that they did not understand when they happened, and took in all the beauty of everything that they sailed past. They especially liked passing the lighthouse at the yacht club and having it blast three horns of recognition at them. All four children, and the two guests that came with Gerri and Gerald, stood at attention and gave a salute to the lighthouse in return. They never knew that their Uncle Derek had set up the whole event with the yacht club commandant, Miles Stanton.

Gerri had difficulty believing that these children onboard Derek's yacht were her same children that she cared for every day. She kept nudging Gerald in the ribs and mouthing the word "wow." Gerald, on the other hand, simply smiled and whispered to her that "enjoy. It won't last forever."

Derek and Stephanie had put together a plan for this three day trip to test some new navigation equipment that Derek had installed, and to give their nieces and nephews an adventure which would include sleeping on the yacht one night, and camping out in a tent another night. Derek and Stephanie's idea of "roughing it" would be sleeping in their stateroom onboard. Gerri and Gerald would handle the onshore, in-the-tent, camping venture with the children and be responsible for cooking the meals and all the other fun parts of camping.

Derek's plan called for them to refuel at the Guilford Yacht Club where they would stay for the first night to sleep. They would then move on up the coastline to the

Rocky Neck State Park where they would pitch their tents on land and stay the second night. Fortunately, the children had a four-day hiatus from school, and the adults were able to clear schedules for four days in the event that they didn't get back in three. It all seemed to come together, and the weather was most cooperative, also.

As the hours rolled by each day, Gerri and Gerald Walker felt more and more bonding and closeness with their four children than they had experienced before. The children liked most everything about the outing except the night they spent in their tents. It was the first time for the children sleeping in sleeping bags, outside, in a tent, and the myriad of sounds that were new and different made for some sleepless hours. When the sun rose the following morning, everyone seemed ready for a few more hours of rest and slumber. Red eyes and yawns were the total greetings for Derek and Stephanie that morning, but no time remained in their schedule for additional naps, or such.

Once breakfast was finished, and clean up completed, it was time to head the 'Stephanie's Joy' west toward Westport, and home.

As Derek captained the yacht expertly through the waters of the Long Island Sound, Gerald and Gerri talked with, and listened to the children's description of their fun adventure. They described how much they like 'yachting', as they called it, and how spending last night in a tent camped out in a state park was both nightmarish and fun. They especially liked hearing lots of new sounds they had never heard before. While all this made for an eerie experience, it provided memories for the children that will last a lifetime.

After securing the yacht securely at their dock, Derek and Stephanie enlisted everyone's help in cleaning the entire ship, inside and out. Decks were washed and scrubbed with brushes, all ropes were wound and stored, and all chrome parts of the ship were polished and shined to a brilliant luster. All the children liked helping Uncle Derek, or as they now referred to him as "The Captain", make his boat all clean and shiny; up to a point. For the children, it was fun for the first eight minutes, then it became non-fun. To their credit, the children lasted just long enough to get most of the yacht cleaned up; the adults finished the rest of it.

As the group carried duffel bags, bags with food that they had not eaten yet, and some sports equipment from the boat back to the house, they followed the pathway from the dock back up to the house. As they got nearer, and nearer the house, a pungent smell of rotting meat became very noticeable and began to have the children feigning sickness. Derek looked at Gerald and gave him a motion with his head as if to say "why don't you and I go investigate before the women and children get any closer."

With that, the men sat down all the items that they had been carrying back from the yacht, asked the wives to keep the children with them there, and wait for the two men to come back after checking the house out.

Derek retrieved a flashlight from his duffel, gave another flashlight to Gerald and started walking toward the Victorian. Gerald gave a quick glance at his children, and gave Gerri a wink of one eye, and followed along after Derek. As the two men walked closer to the Victorian, the odor of rotting meat got stronger and stronger until both men had to cover their noses with handkerchiefs.

As the men reached the rear porch area, Derek suggested that they go in opposite directions around the house and check for any broken windows, or other signs of forced entry before going inside. They then parted company in different directions, shining the beams of their flashlights on every window, door handle, and part of the old house that could possibly be a point of access. The more ground they covered, the less evidence they found that a forced entry had occurred. When they met, again, at the rear porch, Gerald confirmed to Derek that he had not found any sign of forced entry, nor any damage to the house.

Suddenly the ground began to shake and continued for six to seven seconds before stopping. At the same moment the rotting meat smell disappeared and everything went very, very quiet. No sounds of water in the river lapping up against the seawall, no birds chirping or making their sounds, no traffic noise, no sounds, at all, could be heard. It was as if everyone had instantly put on those 'noise-cancelling' headphones that people who fly often, love to wear. The silence was deafening and seemed to last a very, very long time. Just when the two men thought that the silence might go on *ad infinitum,* Gerald's youngest daughter called out in the darkness "Daddy, can we go to bed? I'm tired."

That question seemed to bring life back, as the few night birds began their chirping, and, once again, the river had movement, and sound, as it pushed its' way toward the bay. Gerald told Derek that he would help get the children settled for the night and bring more equipment indoors from the yacht. Derek agreed and said he would check out the inside of the Victorian to see if anything occurred indoors. With that, Derek unlocked the back door and started into the house while Gerald went back to the women and children to retrieve the duffel bags and equipment that had been dropped there.

With all the duffel bags and equipment picked up off the ground, Derek was ready to proceed with the wives and children toward the house when he heard Derek yell out to him.

"Gerald, drop everything and get in here! NOW!" the tone in Derek's voice seemed very scratchy and strained.

"Stephanie, Gerri, take the children back down to the boat and see if you can fix them some hot chocolate. Do not ask why, do not come any closer to the house!"

"Gerald," Derek continued, "I need you here NOW!"

As Stephanie and Gerri ushered the children back down the pathway toward the yacht, Gerald hurried up the steps, across the rear porch, and into the rear 'mud room' area of the old Victorian. Just beyond the mud room is a large pantry area where Derek stood flipping switches at an electrical junction box. As Derek flipped additional switches, without any success, he shone the beam of his flashlight onto Gerald as he walked into the mud room.

"All lights are out and all electricity is off, and something terrible has happened here while we were away," Derek said to Gerald. "I saw a body laying on the floor in a pool of blood that looks like Johnny, and I'm not getting any response from Mr. Walker upstairs. Can you check the electrical wires outside and see if they may have been cut, or something, for me? I need to phone the police and get them out here." Derek looked at the still body laying just five to six feet away, and knew from the darkened silhouette completely motionless and lifeless, that it was Johnny Hamilton. All Derek could do was to stand staring at the silhouette as he fished his iPhone out of his pocket and dialed the police department.

As Derek was describing the scene to an officer on the

phone, Gerald came back into the pantry area saying that the electrical wires have been shorted out somehow and there is no way that he can figure out how to get electricity going, again. With that, Derek told the police officer that they needed the power company to send out workmen to restore power to his house as someone had cut all power and they were completely in the dark. As Derek was about to finish his phone call, he saw flashing red and blue lights from outside the house being bounced off the kitchen walls. Just then, he and Gerald heard someone moving upstairs; as if they had fallen and were trying to get up again. Before Derek could make a move to go find the stairway, two police officers, with their guns drawn and very bright flashlights in hand, came through the back door yelling "don't move! Put your hands up and turn and face the other direction!" Derek knew that he had seen this scene in a movie not too long ago, but decided to comply completely when a second, very stern sounding, voice yelled out "turn around! NOW!"

With that, the police officers asked for identification from Derek and Gerald and why they were here in the dark. After both men showed their ID's, and Derek explained that this is his house and they had just returned from several days away. They had been out of town on a group outing, and that both of their wives, and Gerald's children, were huddled together on the boat tied up at Derek's dock.

As two more uniformed officers arrived at the back door, the group heard the noise coming from upstairs that

Derek and Gerald had heard previously. One of the officers, with Sergeant stripes on his shirt sleeves, used his gun as a pointer tool to signal Derek and Gerald that he wanted them to turn around and face the wall once again. When that was completed, he told the two arriving officers to check out the upper floors to see who, or what, was making the noise. The two officers clicked on their flashlights and went off on their search, carefully stepping over, and around the bloodied areas on the kitchen floor.

Derek kept thinking about how good this event would be when he turned it into a segment of one of his next novels; he would use his first-hand experience to 'juice-up' some parts of his storyline. He was also concerned about the women and Gerald's children waiting on board his boat and not knowing what was happening here at his house. He wanted to ask one of the policemen to check on everyone on his boat, but decided that he would leave that thought unspoken. Just a couple minutes later, another pair of uniformed police officers arrived, and the police Sergeant asked them to go down to the yacht and check on the women and children and see if anyone, other that two wives and the four children, was on board. He reminded them not to disclose anything about what had happened, or was currently happening, at the house.

Just as the two policemen left for the yacht, a crew from North American Power arrived to work on the power outage problem and set about posting their flashing amber warning lights, and signs, that safety regulations required. Five minutes later, two ambulances arrived at the same time as a crew of crime scene investigators from Bridgeport. Suddenly Derek's stately old Victorian Keeper House, had seemingly more people scurrying about than might be present during a Walker family get-together.

The two officers, dispatched by the police Sergeant to investigate sounds coming from upstairs, came back down to report to the Sergeant that there were two elderly people up on the third floor: an elderly woman who was recovering from a fainting episode, and an elderly and badly beaten man who needed medical attention right away.

Derek told the police Sergeant that they were his in-laws, and Gerald's parents, and that Gerald is a medical doctor very familiar with their medical history and should go examine them immediately. The police Sergeant simply looked at Derek for several seconds before asking Gerald if that statement was true. Gerald acknowledged that he is, in fact, an MD with offices in New Haven and was visiting his brother-in-law Derek, and his sister Stephanie, who is Derek's wife. He also confirmed that the elderly couple upstairs are his parents and are living here while their home is being built over on the northwest corner of Derek's property. Gerald offered to show business cards to confirm his medical credentials, but the Sergeant decided to remove the handcuffs from Gerald's wrists and allow him to accompany the medical crew from one of the ambulances upstairs to check the well-being of his parents. The Sergeant also had the handcuffs removed from Derek's wrists just as a policeman arrived from visiting Derek's yacht. The officer confirmed to the Sergeant the identities of the two woman, and that there are four small children with them and that they had just returned from a cruise, and camping, excursion with these two men being questioned.

As Gerald carefully walked around the dead body, avoiding all little pools of blood on the floor, he saw that the deceased person was, indeed, Johnny Hamilton and said so to the Sergeant. This confirmation, of course, brought dozens more questions from the police Sergeant and the crime scene investigators who had recently arrived and were trying to catch up on the flow of information.

Derek informed the Sergeant that Johnny Hamilton had recently sold his home in Bridgeport and was staying with he and his wife Stephanie until he found another, smaller, house to purchase. As the investigators took more, and more information down, the Sergeant told everyone to settle in, that "tonight's going to be a very, very long night."

Just then, the lights came back on in the stately Victorian, and every electrical appliance began singing their nearly-quiet songs: humming along with the refrigerator.

CHAPTER 12

Tom Kitchen opened his eyes in the all-white environment with sounds of people scurrying about and metal clanging on other metal. He looked at a completely white surface in front of him and wondered why he was soaking wet. He knew exactly where he was, and what was going on; NOT! Tom had no idea where he was, or what he was doing. He tried moving his head for a better view of his surroundings but had to stop abruptly due to a severe pain in his neck. He thought for a moment about trying to raise himself up and looking around, but decided against that idea, also. As Tom tried to focus better, and feel more awake, he became aware of how warm and uncomfortable he was becoming. As streams of perspiration ran down his face from his forehead, he felt pains in both arms and realized that he was restrained from moving his arms and hands.

He attempted to call out, not knowing who he would reach, but was unable to because of a very sore throat and very dry mouth. He tried to collect saliva in his mouth to alleviate the dryness in his throat, but none seemed to form. As he attempted a second time to call out, a nurse walked up to his left side and looked down at him.

"Well there, Mr. Kitchen, you got 'dem boilers firing up your temperature, again. Y'all sweatin' like a roasting chunk of meat. I'll get your doctor right away," the nurse said as she exited the room. Boilers? Sweating? Temperature up? Tom was trying to digest these terms when a man in a white coat came to his bedside and asked a nurse on his other side of the bed to mop his face and take his temperature.

"How do you feel, Mr. Kitchen?" asked the young doctor. "Do you know where you are and what is going on?" Tom tried to answer 'no', but was not able to form words and speak. He licked his dry, parched lips several times before the doctor asked the nurse to get some water and a straw for him. The water was refreshing, but did not help Tom speak yet. He tried to get the doctor's face better focused but Tom's eyes were very hot and perspiration kept running into them and making them burn.

Finally, the doctor took a clean towel from the nurse and wiped all the perspiration off Tom's face and away from his eyes so that he could begin to see clearer. Tom struggled to say to the doctor "thank you." The sound of his own voice made Tom wonder who this stranger is that has this weak, unusual-sounding voice and what happened to the one that Tom remembered.

"Where am I?" Tom asked as he saw more and more objects become clearer and sharper.

"You are at St. Vincent Medical Center and you have been very, very sick. We wondered at times if we would ever be talking to you again. You contracted a very dangerous blood poisoning, possible caused either by some wood splinters under your skin, or from some black, powder-like, substance that appears to be gunpowder. We're not sure which. A secondary infection, much like malaria, really complicated both our treatment and a quick recovery from your illnesses." The doctor told Tom. "You were completely out of it for a while, and we had to restrain your arms and hands to protect yourself, and the nursing staff trying to take your temperature and get blood draws. Nothing you did was intentional, just the crazy high temperatures that you were running." The doctor listened to Tom's heart for a moment before checking his mouth and eyes. The nurse gave the doctor Tom's temperature and left the room.

"Tom, do you understand everything I've been telling you?" asked the doctor as he removed the wrist, and arm, restraints from Tom.

Tom struggled to answer that he did, but much of what the doctor told Tom did not register. Tom drifted in and out of sleep until the nurse returned with his antibiotics and raised the head of his bed up so he could take more liquids with the tablets. While Tom was upright, he surveyed his hospital room and did not see anyone in the adjoining bed. The room, itself, was white, spartan, and very typical of hospital wards everywhere. A wall-mounted TV set was turned off and dark.

Tom drank as much of the liquid that the nurse offered

before drifting off to sleep, again.

The dreams that Tom was having were, to say the least, strange. Weird could be a more accurate word as they varied from Tom swinging from tree-to-tree, like Tarzan would, to running across the molten lava flow of Kilauea volcano before jumping into the ocean. Tom saw himself being chased by hundreds, and hundreds of aborigines who were throwing spears and shooting poison darts at him. Dreams so real that he could feel the darts when they would hit his arms.

One dream had Tom shipwrecked on a distant island and without any provisions, at all. He had to climb trees to harvest coconuts, which eventually stopped being coconuts and turned into volleyballs; volleyballs fill with cotton candy and marshmallows. On this island, Tom had no water to drink, so he had to scale a tall mountain and get beer from a small mountain tavern where all the people inside were from his family. He drifted into, and out of, conscientiousness long enough to see the outline of the doctor bent over him doing something; the doctor always was in silhouette mode and never clearly outlined.

As Tom dreamed, he seemed to always be running from the hordes of aborigines chasing him everywhere. Finally, he dreamed that he found a gun and started shooting at them to get them to stop the chase. Every time he would shoot one, and he would fall down, three more would jump up and resume the chase after Tom. Tom kept running and running until he could not run another step. He turned to face the horde chasing him only to get hit by dozens and dozens of poison darts from their blow guns. As Tom saw himself fall to the ground, the aborigines grabbed his arms and legs and tried running in opposite directions. This caused his limbs to start coming out of their sockets, and Tom could feel himself jerking to get away from them.

Suddenly, Tom awoke. Wide awake and looking clearly at everything in his hospital room. He saw the nurse replacing the fluid bags on the apparatus next to his bed. He saw the monitors with their wavy red, green, and yellow lines and numbers. He watched as the lines did their dances up, down, up again ever changing the corresponding numbers. He saw the other bed in his room which now contained a man who seemed to be connected to the same type of equipment that Tom was. He was now seeing everything clearly and precisely as it is.

When the nurse saw Tom looking around, she smiled and said that she would get the doctor "right away." With that, she hurried out of the room, only to return minutes later with the doctor following behind her.

"Among us living, now?" the doctor asked. He checked Tom's vitals and listened to Tom's heart and lungs. The doctor smiled as he took a step backwards and asked Tom how many fingers he was holding up.

"Three," Tom answered. "Well, actually, two fingers and one thumb."

The doctor laughed and smiled at Tom's response and said, "it's good to have you back with us. Your vitals are looking better than they have in a long, long time and your eyes seem clear and sharp." The doctor made notes in Tom's records and gave some further instructions to the nurse as she left the room.

"Who are you?" Tom asked the doctor. "I mean, what is your name?"

"I'm Dr. Chambers, Tom, and I was working a 'fill-in' shift in the ER when they brought you in. Then you went to ICU when I was working there. Since you were transferred out of ICU, you ended up on my floor. So I figured that we have become some sort of soul mates, or something. Anyway, I am your primary physician until dismissal. How are you feeling? Are you hungry, yet? You haven't had any solid food since last week. How do you feel about eating?"

"Last week?" asked Tom. "Just how long have I been here? What day, or date, is it anyway?"

"Today is Wednesday the ninth. You came into ER thirteen days ago; a very sick, sick fellow."

"The ninth? It can't be!" exclaimed Tom in horror. "I can't have been here almost two weeks. I have businesses to run, I have commitments on the first of the month! Tell me you're mistaken, please."

With that outburst, Dr. Chambers turned on the TV set on the wall and showed Tom that it said 'Wednesday, July 9th' on the screen. "Your admission ticket says you were brought into the ER and into exam room #5 at 10:10 PM on Friday, June 23rd. Since then it has been a real struggle to keep you among the living. The infection was fairly easy to handle, it was the secondary problems with the malaria, and blood poisoning that gave us the problems. How did you come into contact with malaria? That's rarely seen in the United States anymore; especially in our New England region. Were you living in Central, or South America years ago?"

Dr. Chambers slowed for a moment and watched Tom's reaction to all that the doctor had told him so far. "Mr. Kitchen, is there someone that the hospital could call and notify of your improvements? Do you want us to notify anyone of your whereabouts? You did not have any personal information on you when admitted; no contact information, that is."

"Only one that needs immediate contacting is my manager at my hardware store; and, maybe the manager of my jewelry and clock stores. They have been functioning all this time not knowing of my whereabouts." Tom answered. He thought for a few minutes trying to remember phone numbers and became exasperated when the numbers didn't come to mind.

"I may be able to give you business names and locations, but phone numbers and people's names are escaping me right now. Can we talk about this in the morning?" Tom asked the doctor.

"Well, it is morning right now, but we can postpone contacting people until later, or even tomorrow." Dr. Chambers replied.

Tom had been fighting with himself to stay awake, but the need to go to sleep overpowered him finally and he drifted off.

When Tom awoke again, a tray of food sat on a rolling table next to his bed, and a nurse was replacing bottles of liquids on the opposite bed side. He tried to focus on whatever was being shown on the TV set, but was unable to do so. The nurse finished her task, smiled at Tom and went across the room to begin stripping the sheets off the now empty bed.

"My room mate out of the room?" Tom asked the nurse. He watched her as she finished with the last bed covers, put everything into a plastic laundry bag and left the room without answering Tom's question, or, making any comments at all.

"Well, same to you!" Tom thought to himself. He looked around to see if anything else had changed in the few minutes that he had been asleep. Everything else appeared to be as it was.

The head nurse walked into the room and smiled at Tom. "Nice to see you awake, again. Can I have this food warmed up for you, or would you like to have something else to eat?" she asked.

Tom surveyed every item on the food tray before telling the nurse, "I don't like to waste anything, so if this is heated up, I'll eat some of this. Certainly went from hot to cold fast. Didn't it?"

The nurse laughed her full belly laugh and informed Tom that the tray had been alongside his bed almost three hours. No wonder it is a bit cold. Tom couldn't believe the nurses statement and told her that he thought he had only been asleep for a few minutes.

"Mr. Kitchen, sir, you've been 'sleep more than five hours. Not just few minutes." The nurse responded as she picked up the food tray to leave. "I be back little while with your hot food. You drink some water."

Tom asked this nurse about the man who was in the other bed as she was leaving with his food, but did not get any answer from her, either. Tom watched the picture on the TV screen change from a dog food commercial, to an ad for feminine products, to an ad promoting a sale on Summer sporting equipment at a local sporting goods store.

Tom watched everything shift from commercial to commercial and wondered why he wasn't advertising his businesses on television. Businesses? That's right! Someone was going to call people at his businesses for him and inform them where Tom is at; some hospital. Some medical center. But where? He thought. Where?

A young nurse came into the room and asked Tom about adjusting his bed so he would be able to drink, or eat his food when it came back. Tom agreed to have the head of the bed raised up. Just as the young nurse finished getting the bed adjusted to Tom's liking, Dr. Chambers came in the room with a group of eight or nine medical students following right on his heels.

Dr. Chambers introduced Tom to the students and explained Tom's numerous medical problems to them and what the treatment for each has been. The doctor went into details and answered questions from each before throwing out questions for them to answer. The entire visit from the group lasted about fifteen minutes and as they were leaving the room, another nurse brought a food tray in and set it on the table alongside Tom's bed. Tom noticed that it contained new, different food items than had not been on the previous tray, and had two containers of Jello on it. Not one, but TWO! Suddenly Tom was noticeably hungry and was developing a craving for Jello.

Later, when the doctor came in to check on him, Tom

stopped eating and told Dr. Chambers that he was ready to give someone names and phone numbers of people to be contacted. Tom also asked Dr. Chambers when he thought that he would be getting discharged from the hospital. Tom felt that he was, suddenly, feeling great and could leave any time. Not a feeling shared by Dr. Chambers, or other medical personnel.

Dr. Chambers smiled at Tom, and listened to him explaining how wonderful he was feeling. The doctor then reviewed Tom's medical charts before telling him that he still had a high level of poison in his system in addition to his temperature spiking up and down without a cause. The doctor explained all the problems that still plagued Tom and told him that there would not be any consideration for discharge from the hospital for at least 72 hours. This was not what Tom wanted to hear and he got somewhat angry at Dr. Chambers for not allowing him to leave.

Dr. Chambers left Tom's room to head for the stairs so he could make his way upstairs to see more of his patients; primarily, Mr. & Mrs. Walker. Mr. Walker, and a few of his family members, had been injured, or traumatized, during a recent incident at the Keeper House Victorian down in Westport. Carl Walker, and his wife Carla, had been admitted into the hospital for a 48 hour evaluation after learning of the murder of Carla's brother, Johnny Hamilton. Carla had gone into deep, deep shock upon getting the news, and had to be revived by, and transported to the hospital by, EMT's from an ambulance company who responded to the 9-1-1 call. Both of them had already been released and were continuing their recoveries at home.

Mrs. Walker had been deeply traumatized when she returned from a trip to Boston and found her aged husband unconscious from a savage beating, and laying near death on their bedroom floor in the Victorian house. Mr. Walker had been bound onto a wooden chair and pistol-whipped by an unknown assailant until the ER doctors were uncertain whether, or not, Mr. Walker would survive. It was Mrs. Walker who placed the original 9-1-1 call for assistance, but all the Walker family members seemed to take the news about Johnny's murder quite hard. The Walker's oldest daughter, Stephanie Hunter, and Stephanie's husband, Derek, also had to be admitted into the hospital for a couple days treatment and observation. No family member seemed to have escaped the effects of this senseless event.

Of all the family members, Dr. Chambers was most concerned about Mr. Walker. He had received the most brutal of assaults and even had to have facial surgery to repair a badly broken, and dislodged, jaw and cheek. The doctor admired Mr. Walker a great deal; besides being a benefactor of the new Children's wing of the hospital, Dr. Chambers knew that Mr. Walker was an unusually tough individual. But even with Mr. Walker's toughness, he had barely escaped dancing with death from this incident.

Dr. Chambers walked into the Walker's private room, furnished to hospital VIP's by the hospital board. As he entered, he saw Mrs. Walker asleep in the adjoining bed, while Mr. Walker enjoyed sound sleep in his bed. Dr. Chambers walked very softly so he would not disturb either of them and looked over Mr. Walker's medical charts. He liked the stats that he saw and decided he would come back to examine the healing of Mr. Walker's surgery later in the day. For now, everything looked okay and he surmised that Mr. Walker could possibly be released from the hospital in two or three days. Later, closer examination of him would confirm that.

As Dr. Chambers left the Walker's room, he stopped at the nurse's station and looked up the other Walker family members in the computer system. He wanted to make certain that all the others had been released and that Mr. & Mrs. Walker were the only remaining family members still in the hospital. Then, having put his mind at ease, it was on to making rounds of his other patients.

The next couple of days were pretty routine and relatively quiet for Dr. Chambers. After getting Tom's surgeon to examine him, and getting his approval for discharge, Dr. Chambers read the final stats concerning Tom's vitals, checked the latest lab report and then told Tom that he could go home. News that Tom had been waiting for several days to hear. Now that he had finally heard it, he wasn't sure what he wanted: to stay longer where he was safe and cared for, or go back to reality and see how his world had gotten along without him. He debated the choices in his mind, but knew he had only one choice: back to reality.

Tom got dressed, got his plastic envelope containing his personal items such as keys, money, and wallet. Got his list of medicines and follow up doctor appointments, and final instructions from his nurse. All Tom had left to do was to stop by the discharge desk and sign himself out. Once all his paperwork was done, and insurance papers signed, Tom asked the lady behind the counter to call a taxi for him; he was going home.

Dr. Chambers was very pleased with how well Mr. Walker had recovered and his plastic surgeon was giving the 'green light' to his being released. Mrs. Walker was probably the most pleased and relieved about her husband's recovery and the appearance of his face after the brutal beating. Several operations had to be done to get Mr. Walker's shattered cheek and jaw reconstructed, and skin had to be taken from various locations on his body and grafted onto his face to replace skin lost during the beating. Mr. Walker was leaving the hospital with his jaw still wired shut, but he was happy to be going home even though he knew he might relive the beating over and over again.

Dr. Chambers, and the plastic surgeon, gave final instructions to Mrs. Walker, and to daughter Stephanie, on what Mr. Walker will require, in the way of care, after he leaves the hospital. A schedule, and routine for medications and feeding procedures was outlined with special attention given to feeding. With his jaw still being held in place with wire, feeding will require patience and loving care. Both women understood the type of care needed.

Mr. Walker had written a note to Stephanie that when they get home, he wants to get his iPad charged fully so that he did not have to be writing notes to everyone all the time. His inability to be able to speak to everyone would be the hardest thing Mr. Walker would have to endure. Pain, medications, having to have everything he consumes in liquid form, and everything else, would seem minor to not be able to talk and eat properly.

With Mr. Walker safely in a wheelchair, being handled by a head nurse, they all entered the elevator to go down to the main floor. They crossed the lobby of the main floor to await Derek's arrival with the car. Mr. Walker was busy listening to his wife and daughter talk to each other, and wishing that he could talk to them to tell them to look at how beautiful the day is. The sun shining, warm breeze gently blowing around and through the portico of the hospital entrance. Birds were flying all around outside and the warm gentle breezes seemed to give them lift and energy to fly even more.

Mr. Walker was enjoying just watching the birds fly by,

and children running after each other on the lawn area when he saw something he couldn't believe! There, he was certain, was the man who broke into the Victorian, attacked and beat him nearly to death.

Suddenly Mr. Walker was very agitated and waving his hands and arms and pointing toward the portico and trying to make sounds which would make words. He raised up out of his wheelchair which brought a scolding from the nurse and had both Stephanie and Mrs. Walker trying to gently push him back into his seat. He kept waving his arms and pounding on Mrs. Walker's arm and pointing to the outside.

"No, we are not taking a taxi, Derek is bringing the car around front and he will take us back to the house." Mrs. Walker told her husband. Mrs. Walker looked out front again and saw the taxi slowly pull away from the hospital and move quickly down the street until it was out of sight. Mr. Walker remained very upset and waving his arms and making a motion with his hand as if he was writing something; or, wanting to write something.

Stephanie watched her father and finally asked him if he wanted a pencil and paper. Mr. Walker shook his head "yes." With that, Stephanie took a pen and paper out of her purse and gave it to her father.

Mr. Walker looked outside several times before he started writing *'just saw man who beat me* with gun get into taxi and leave hospital.'

Stephanie and Mrs. Walker read the note as Mr. Walker was writing it and stood staring at each other before Stephanie asked her father if he was sure. Mr. Walker shook his head 'yes' and pointed to the front door of the hospital just as Derek was walking through it.

Derek stopped and looked behind him as if Mr. Walker was pointing at something that Derek had not seen. Then Derek continued on inside and said "hi" to everyone.

"Derek, did you see a man get into a taxi out front as you were pulling up?" asked Stephanie. "My father said he saw the man who beat him up so badly leave the hospital and get into a taxi out front."

"There was a taxi picking up someone, but I was finishing a phone call with my office and Daniel Thornton, the author, so I did not see who got into the taxi." Derek replied.

Derek looked at his father-in-law and asked him if he was sure that it was the same man. Mr. Walker shook his head 'yes' again, and wrote "it was dark in the room when I heard someone on the

KEEPER OF THE KEY

stairs. Just as he opened the bedroom door, I turned the light on and got a full, face-on view of him before he hit me with the gun. I hit the bedroom floor, tried to get up, and got another view of his face before he hit me again and I passed out."

Stephanie asked her father if the police had asked him whether or not he could identify the assailant. Mr. Walker said that he did not remember being asked. The nurse reminded Stephanie that her father still suffered from a mild form of amnesia and will have difficulty remembering things for some time, yet. The nurse recommended lots and lots of patience in letting his brain recover in its' own speed and time.

As the group waited for Derek to return, a young woman dressed in business casual attire, and wearing a windbreaker jacket with a 'CNN' logo on it, approached them. "Good afternoon, Ladies, and Mr. & Mrs. Walker." She said "I am Janice Wilkins from CNN. We met some time back at the dedication of the Children's Hospital wing and I asked about doing an interview with you and your husband, regarding the history of your Victorian house down in Westport. Now, however, I have been told that the Walkers were victims of an attack, and possible pistol whipping, while residing in your Victorian. Can I get any statements regarding this report?"

Stephanie went into a quick legal-defense mode before telling the young reporter, "I do not know where you get your information, whether it's from off-the-street gossip, or from one of those so-called 'gossip' newspapers like the National Reporter, but your information is wrong. This accident didn't happen at our home. Now, if you will excuse us we have to get my parents home and my father needs rest."

"I fully understand, Mrs. Hunter, but I have very good sources, and they have told me that an intruder broke into your home, the Keeper House, and your father, Mr. Walker, surprised him and for that, Mr. Walker got beat up quite badly. Now, if any of that is not the truth, please let me know. Now."

Mrs. Walker had been standing by, listening before telling Stephanie, " Ms. Wilkins should get some correct information regarding what happened to your father, and, maybe she, with her resources can help to find the man who did this."

"Thank you, Mrs. Walker, but it's MRS. Wilkins."

"Very sorry, Mrs. Wilkins, but we have had a very traumatic experience and are not quite settled down yet. But Stephanie, Mrs. Wilkins was kind enough to write several very nice, and very good, articles about the efforts being put forth to fund and build the children's hospital. Then she wrote a very nice feature article on your father and I and our helping to get the hospital built. Perhaps she is someone who can be helpful, and be trusted."

Stephanie looked at her mother with one eyebrow raised. "Articles written? Feature article on you and Daddy? I thought she said she is with CNN. The cable news network."

Janice Wilkins sensed the questions running through lawyer Stephanie's mind and quickly told her that in addition to being employed by CNN, that she is a contributing reporter for the New York Times, and the Hartford Courant. Janice focuses mostly on special topics, and local subjects for her articles for the two newspapers.

Mrs. Walker took a card from her purse, wrote something on the back and handed it to Janice Wilkins. "This is our home phone number. Call me tomorrow afternoon some time and let's find a day and time that we can get together for tea and talk. Perhaps we each can help the other in some ways. Will you do that?"

Janice Wilkins smiled at Mrs. Walker as she took the card and put it in a jacket pocket. She confirmed that she would be phoning tomorrow afternoon and thanked everyone for their time as she turned to walk off toward the discharge desk.

Derek, who had gone outside the entry doors to see if he could see the taxi going down the street, came back inside and told the nurse that he would take the wheelchair out to the car. The nurse thank him and told Derek that it is hospital policy that all discharged patients must be taken 'curbside' by a hospital employee; insurance company rules.

With that, the nurse gently pushed the wheelchair across the hospital foyer and through the entry doors to the waiting car. The nurse and Stephanie helped Mr. & Mrs. Walker into the rear seat as Derek started the engine and then proceeded to drive everyone back to Keeper House.

Tom got home and immediately read the instructions on his many discharge papers, got all his medications together, and went about setting up a routine for his medicines. Once everything was arranged to Tom's satisfaction, he took the first group of medicines and went to get ready for bed; he knew he needed more sleep and rest before he jumped back into business matters.

It was just over eleven hours later when Tom awoke feeling rested and refreshed and wishing he had a cup of coffee in his hand already. He stretched a bit and thought about how warm he felt; as if he still had a slight fever. He fixed himself a cup of coffee and was about to phone his manager of the hardware store when he realized that it was not yet seven o'clock in the morning. Tom decided he would get cleaned up and go visit his businesses and thank his people for keeping things going while he was hospitalized.

Tom found things very much to his liking at both his jewelry store, and the clock shop. Both stores had received word of Tom's hospitalization, and the managers had gone about business as usual. Profits up! Everything good! Tom thought to himself that maybe he needs to be hospitalized more often to increase profits.

The opposite was true at the Ace Hardware store: shipments of 'sale' inventory items had not been received on time, some items which had been received were defective and had to be returned, and a group of three individuals had decided to rob the store, customers and employees, at gunpoint about a week ago. Tom had difficulty believing that so many bad things could have happened in such a short period of time; but knowing they had, he went to work to get everything back on an even keel.

Tom got concerned, as he worked, about his increasing temperature and lack of energy. He mopped his forehead repeatedly to keep perspiration out of his eyes, and had to pause and rest for a few minutes, every fifteen minutes, or so. Tom read the police report of the robbery as he waited on hold to speak to the head of the Ace Distribution Center.

Tom knew how to handle the returning of merchandise since he had handled it for so many years with good results. He had met the man, who now managed the center, years ago and developed a close friendship which allowed Tom to pick up the phone and ask for a favor. Something that few others enjoyed.

As Tom read the police report of the robbery, one thing kept jumping out at him: the description of the robbers was repeatedly given as "Hispanic, or Latino males, approx. six feet tall with each having a unique tattoo on the left side of their necks." Tom was thinking about that portion of the report as he wiped perspiration from his forehead and tried to remember why it bothered him. "That's it!" Tom told himself. "That's the thing that I'm seeing. It's that damn description that's eating at me!" Hispanic males. Six feet tall. Unique tattoo on the left side of their necks. Mendoza Mob! "It has to be!" Tom told himself.

'Mendoza Mob' brought new chills to Tom's body, not to mention fear running up his spine. Why, if it was really them, would they suddenly appear at his hardware store? Why would they resort to robbing hardware....? "OH, MY GOD!!" Tom thought out loud. "Oh, my God! How could I forget that? How could I forget to make the payment to Ernesto? How could I put my brother George in jeopardy this way?" The thoughts were racing through Tom's mind and they helped to raise his temperature higher, and higher. Suddenly Tom also remembered that he had sent a coded message to his sister before going into the hospital. He found his iPhone and was hot surprised to find that it was completely dead. No juice left! Tom dropped the police report on his desk and quickly plugged his iPhone in to begin charging it so he could check for a response.

Tom tried phoning Ernesto Siguenya to explain why he was not able to make the deposit to his Canadian bank account on the first of the month. Tom had hopes that Ernesto would understand and allow Tom to make a late deposit, even if it cost Tom some additional money for interest. As the phone rang and rang, Tom kept his fingers crossed that Ernesto would be understanding; otherwise he did not know what effect this would have on brother George. The phone continued to ring until a recording said "away from phone, leave your number' in a heavy male Latin voice. Tom left a quick message with his name and phone number to call back to.

Tom combed through a drawer full of papers in his desk trying to find a business card for Ernesto which had another number that he could be reached at. When Tom finally found it, he placed the call quickly, only to hear that the 'number you are calling is no longer in service" message. Now Tom was getting concerned; he was also perspiring like a roasting pig on a BBQ spit. As he wiped lots of perspiration from his forehead, he wished that he had remembered to bring his medications with him as he was due to take another batch of pills.

Tom's manager came into Tom's office to discuss the police report, and the insurance claim that needs to be filed with the insurance company. As they discussed the list of items taken during the robbery, which was almost totally comprised of money, Tom continued to perspire more and more. Finally, Tom's manager stopped talking and asked Tom if he thought he should go home and rest; he was not looking well and was perspiring profusely. Tom assured him that he was okay to continue on with the business talk, and then he might leave.

Tom's manager informed him that the reporter from CNN came back a couple days after they saw her here last time, for their interview pertaining to small businesses and the Connecticut coastal business environment. The manager apologized to her saying that he did not know, at that time, where Tom was at; he had left the store for his appointment, that day, and had not been seen or heard from since. Tom thanked his manager for handling that situation and said how sorry he was that the hospital did not contact Tom's important people with his whereabouts. Tom also expressed his great appreciation for the manager handling everything else that needed doing while Tom was in the hospital recovering. Tom assured him that there would be "something very special" in his paycheck next payday.

The two men continued discussing store related problems for another ten minutes before Tom decided that he had done as much as he could do for one day. It was now time for Tom to go home and medicate. With that, Tom said his fair wells as his manager handed Tom a business card from Janice Wilkins from CNN. Tom said he would take care of CNN when he felt a little better. He grabbed some papers and put them into a folder, grabbed some reports that his bookkeeper had prepared for him last week, and checked his iPhone which was still on the charger. He smiled to himself when he saw a coded response from his sister, but quickly got concerned when he saw the reply was twelve days old. Twelve days old. This meant that Tom had to start all over again as, the way things had been conceived a long time ago, when one of them contacted another, you had to reply within forty-eight hours or everything went back to square one. Tom was back to square one.

Tom left the hardware store and hurried home to medicate. By now he was feeling tired, very achy and like he was getting sick all over again. He continued to perspire quite heavily and by the time he walked into his home, his vision was no longer clear and sharp. He found his medications and quickly swallowed the proper mixture of pills. Although Tom was feeling a little hunger, he knew that he had better lay down for a short nap before attempting anything else.

Off to dreamland.

CHAPTER 13

With upcoming doctor's appointments for both Mr. and Mrs. Walker, partners' meetings and meetings with clients, for Stephanie, and demands for Derek to be in the City for several days conducting business, it was decided that they all would meet with Janice Wilkins from CNN as soon as she could make it to Keeper House. As they soon discovered, that would be tomorrow; at the Victorian for lunch and conversation.

While Mr. Walker was recuperating in the hospital, Derek hired a contractor to do repairs to the Victorian so that when they returned home, it was as if nothing had ever happened. All signs of the assault on Mr. Walker, and of the murder of Johnny Hamilton were completely erased. It took some time before the police department would allow the crime scene to be disturbed, but the contractor worked fast and completed everything quickly once Derek got approval. Derek also had a 'three-person' elevator installed which runs from the first floor directly up to the third floor. Stephanie knew that both of her parents would appreciate this feature, especially when Mrs. Walker has to run upstairs to attend to her husband.

The following day they all were downstairs for breakfast except for Mr. Walker, who had not slept well the night before. He tossed and turned and kept his wife awake much of the night, also.

After finishing cleaning up from breakfast, Stephanie and Mrs. Walker prepared food and got ready for the luncheon with Janice Wilkins. Stephanie felt something light and simple should satisfy everyone's appetite. Mrs. Walker also fixed some liquid food that she could feed to her husband when he got hungry. Mr. Walker's mouth and jaw being wired shut was not helping improve his disposition.

Janice Wilkins arrived exactly on time along with her cameraman named Elliott, whom Janice called 'Eli'. After introductions to everyone, Eli looked for a good place to set up his lighting and camera equipment for the video portion of the interview.

After a guided tour of the house, Eli voted for the family room area as it had good, natural, light and ample lamps for any additional lighting needed. He set up the video camera, light bouncers, his tripod, and other equipment needed for his 'shoot', but had to go back to his truck in the driveway for some cords that he needed.

Janice Wilkins started talking to Mrs. Walker about why she and her husband were living here instead of their estate on Long Island. Mrs. Walker gave Janice the short version of the story as she saw a light begin to flash on a pendant that she wore around her neck. The flashing light meant that her husband was summoning her and had pushed a button upstairs to signal her. Mrs. Walker excused herself and headed off to the newly-installed elevator to go up to the third floor.

Janice then directed her interview to Derek and Stephanie with a lengthy list of questions about their Victorian. Questions from "what made you buy this particular house," to why they decided to leave Long Island, "were you told the history behind this Victorian," to how long Janice Wilkins has been researching Keeper House and its' history. The more that they talked about the Victorian, the more uneasy Stephanie became; she did not know how much Janice Wilkins knew about the 'events' that went on occasionally. Events like the rotting meat odor, the very low growling sounds that the house made, as well as the ground-shaking, rumbling that goes on sometimes. Finally, Janice asked question after question and got a lot of information, but was not certain that she was getting ALL the facts and information from Stephanie and Derek.

After several minutes of talking, the lawyer in Stephanie 'kicked in' when she asked Janice "why have you been researching the Keeper House, and for how long? It certainly is not 'main-stream' news for CNN."

After the question, it was obvious to Stephanie that Janice was mentally searching for the correct way for her to answer. Finally, Janice decided to face this session head-on and let this nice couple know what she knows. Janice looked at Eli and told him to turn the recorders off and have a comfortable seat for awhile. She told him that there would be a lot of "off-the-record talk going on for a while" and he didn't need to worry about getting it recorded.

Janice then looked at Stephanie and Derek and told them "I'll try to keep this as short as possible, but even at that it is going to last awhile."

Stephanie asked her if she would like a glass of wine or some other beverage to drink before she started. Janice thanked her and asked for a glass of red wine. Derek got up and poured all of them each a glass of his favorite Cabernet.

Janice took the glass from Derek, thanked him, took a sip of the red wine as she began her story. "I first heard about Keeper House while doing undergrad studies at NYU, where I ran into Jeff Eldon the youngest son of Dr. Helen Eldon. Jeff was a freshman and just sort of bouncing around, not knowing what he was doing or where he was headed. We had a first year Creative Writing class together and would see each other in the commons. We were both guests at a frat party one evening, and it was obvious that Jeff had been drinking a lot. A lot! He started talking about how evil his life was, and I just thought it was the alcohol talking. I didn't even ask him any questions about why he thought his life was evil; he just kept talking to me after telling me that I had to swear myself to secrecy. I laughed to myself, but could tell that even in his drunken state that he was serious. He told me about a big, evil event that went on inside a Victorian mansion where his mother and her siblings lived as children. He told me his mother's birth name was Jessup, but she was adopted by the Keeper family, and raised as if she had always been one of theirs.

It was during a family outing, a church function or something like that, that all the family got together in the living room of Keeper House along with an Uncle's family who had come over. The two families were so identical to each other that it was eerie: husband and wife almost the same age and size, and both had two boys and two girls. All children were the same ages and looked very similar to each other." Janice took another long drink of the delicious Cabernet. She smiled at Stephanie and continued. "Someone broke into the Victorian and began shooting family members. Father, Mother, children were all victims of the mass execution going on inside Keeper House. When the shooting stopped, and the smoke cleared somewhat, the entire Keeper family had been murdered. They all lain together in a huge pool of crimson, red, blood. Blood that Jeff said seemed to flow like a country stream wanting to build itself into a huge river. Blood that covered a large area of the living room floor." Janice slowly looked in the direction of the living room for a few seconds before continuing, "whoever murdered all those people did not realize that the Keeper children were upstairs on the second floor watching everything through the banister of the stairway and saw the faces of everyone involved. The children could identify the killers!" Janice said.

At this point Derek's writer's instincts took over and his sixth sense had him scratching his head and asking "this just sounds a bit bizarre, don't you think? Someone comes into this house, knows the family is here, starts shooting every man, woman and child and doesn't notice that they are murdering the wrong people. You don't find that strange? I really wonder about his story. I really do"

Stephanie agreed with her husband and said that this type of 'evidence' would not hold up in a court case. She, too, was questioning all of this story that this Jeff Eldon was telling under a condition of inebriation; Stephanie was not feeling that this was uncovering anything new that they wanted to know.

Janice went on to tell them of the many hours of research that she had done, mostly because she wanted to DIS-prove the story that Jeff Eldon had told her. The more investigation that she did, the more credible his story started sounding. She decided to drop her research and forget abound invalidating Jeff's tale. She did not do anything more regarding the Keeper family murders, or Keeper House until she was transferred from the Charlotte, North Carolina office, up to the Boston office. She was assigned to investigate reports of a Russian 'spy ship' cruising off the coast of the United States and creeping into the Long Island Sound during the dead of night.

Janice went to New Haven to interview people who supposedly knew about the spy ship and after two days was able to determine that whatever ship may have been spotted, it was long gone. During Janice's many hours of interviewing people, she did get some 'leads' on people who had spotted a Russian submarine in the Thames River region of New London, Connecticut. Now this sounded like just another 'UFO sighting' to Janice until she talked with a husband and wife who were visiting relatives in New Haven. The older couple lived in the Groton Heights district and she worked part-time at Paul's Pasta Shop, an Italian eatery right alongside the Thames River. Her account of her sighting of this "alien submarine thing" was very exact, very precise. Even though it happened after she got off work, she could see the ship perfectly and describe every detail. Her husband, it turns out is an ex-submariner from the U.S. Navy and knows subs very well. He is also a volunteer at the U.S. Submarine World War II Veterans Memorial, and was working late with other volunteers, repairing some vandalism that had occurred at the memorial. When the group of volunteers finally finished their tasks, her husband left and went south on Thames Street, where they live. As he got within a couple blocks of Paul's Pasta Shop where his wife worked, he saw a sub break the surface of the Thames River briefly. This is nothing unusual as New

London is the home to the U.S. Navy's Naval Submarine Base.

The husband immediately noticed that the sub he saw break the surface, and was now submerging again, did not have the silhouette of a U.S. Navy sub. The 'conning tower' structure was much longer and larger than is typical of our subs, he told Janice, and it contained many more antennas than we would be likely to have. He could not swear that it was a Russian sub, but he knew it was not a U.S. sub. Both the husband and wife reported their sightings to U.S. Navy authorities, who dismissed it as "nothing. Nothing at all."

Janice said that she was interested in checking out this report in New London, but received information about a 'sighting' off the coast in Westport. Not knowing exactly where Westport was at, she headed southwest until she got close and left I-95. It was late at night when Janice arrived in Westport, and she wasn't certain exactly where she was at. She looked for a motel to get a room for the night but did not find one; Janice was definitely in an upscale residential area. It was late and she was very tired and afraid that if she went on any more, she would fall asleep at the wheel of her car.

She found a large lot in a quiet area that was bordered by tall trees and she parked her car. Feeling extreme fatigue, her body aching from prolonged activity without rest, and her eyes feeling like each one had a five pound weight attached to it, she turned off the cars' engine, locked all her doors, and feel asleep.

She awoke early in the morning to someone knocking on the window of her car. She rubbed her eyes and looked to see a uniformed police officer standing along side her car telling her to "roll down your car window." She complied and began telling the office about how lost she became last night, how very tired she was, and how to avoid crashing into something with her car, she pulled over to rest. She showed the officer her business card and her driver's license, and listened to the officer scold her for such a dangerous thing to do. He gave her directions on how to get back to I-95, tipped his hat to her and left the area.

Janice said that she needed to walk a bit to work the kinks out of her legs and then she needed food, and coffee. As she walked down the road a few yards she came to the end of the row of trees. As she looked off to her left she saw a beautiful, three-story, well-maintained Victorian mansion. A Victorian house exactly like the one that Jeff Eldon had described to her years ago. EXACTLY! Every little detail, the color, the location on the property, everything was, as inebriated Jeff had described it. But how could this be, she wondered; how could she drive to a city that she had never been to before, get lost, and, from extreme tiredness park fifty yards away from THIS Victorian?

Janice hurried to start her car and drive away, she told Derek and Stephanie. She felt she had to get away and find a different place in Westport. She headed back Stony Point Road until she found a café that was open.

She ordered coffee and breakfast and used their restroom to freshen up in.

As she finished her third cup of coffee, she said she was beginning to feel human again. She chatted with the young waitress about the area quite some time before asking her if she knew about the big Victorian mansion at the end of Stony Point Road.

"That's an evil, evil place. There was a mass murder there many years ago. Whole family killed including the kids. Still rumored that some spooky things happen there. I wouldn't go there if I was you." The young waitress said as she poured more coffee.

Just then, Mrs. Walker came into the room and asked if anyone was going to eat lunch, or not. She told Eli, Janice Wilkins cameraman, that they had made a selection of sandwiches, had salads also, and some apple pie for desert. She invited everyone to join her in the dining room and she would get the food. Stephanie excused herself to go assist Mrs. Walker with lunch and asked Derek to show Eli and Janice to the dining room.

Janice went on to finish her story and then began

asking question again about the house. She had not heard why Derek and Stephanie ended up buying this house, or how much they knew about the Keeper family murders. They spent another hour while eating talking about the why, the when, and the other facts pertaining to the purchase of the Keeper House mansion.

After lunch was over, Stephanie served pie and hot tea to everyone and asked if Janice and Eli wanted to see the living room where the murders were supposed to have happened.

Janice said she would like to see the living room and asked Eli to go get the camera and bring it along. Eli jumped up from his chair and went back to the family room. When he went to retrieve the camera off the tripod he had used, he saw that it had never turned off, but had continued to record, and then gone dead. Eli quickly put a new battery pack in the camera, replaced the hard drive with a new one with ample recording space, checked the camera to make certain everything was operating like it is supposed to, and made his way out to the living room.

When Eli walked into the living room, Derek was pulling their area rug back to expose the dark brown stained area on the wooden floor boards. Eli started recording and was amazed at how large the stained area is. Janice looked around the room; something did not seem right to her. She laid on the floor and looked all around including looking out toward the stairway. She felt that things were missing and nothing was adding up correctly. Janice asked Derek if they had done any remodeling in this room and heard that they had done extensive remodeling to most of the first floor rooms.

Janice talked to Derek about remodeling done to the living room and decided that things that Jeff Eldon had told her years ago, could not be verified now. Janice asked Derek about changes that may have been made to the wall between the living room and Derek's office. Derek said that the wall was original, and that no alterations or changes had been made to it at all. That information puzzled Janice because if this was the original wall, there was not enough of a sight line between the second floor and the living room.

Janice asked Derek if he remembered a large rectangle, maybe twelve inches square, on the north wall. She wasn't real sure exactly where it would have been located, but somewhere on the north wall. Derek thought for several minutes before shaking his head no.

Stephanie reminded Derek about the square marked on that wall that she asked him about before the contractor covered over it with vinyl wall covering. Stephanie was studying the wall to see if she could now locate where the square was at. She studied, and studied before walking over to a spot between a chair and love seat to get a close-up look. The more Stephanie studied the wall, the less certain she was that she could locate the exact spot.

Derek, too, went over to feel around on the wall in another area. He hoped that he might feel something under the beautiful vinyl that Stephanie had installed, but was not able to lend anything to their search for the square.

It was finally decided that there was not enough time left to continue feeling around to try to locate this square, and that Derek or Stephanie might continue looking for it at another time.

Stephanie asked Janice Wilkins why this square area on this particular wall was of such great importance. Janice admitted that she didn't know, exactly, but that Jeff Eldon had made a 'big deal' out of it and kept saying that he had to get back to Westport, and the square on the wall, many times. He talked about it as though it was a compulsion with him, and Janice wondered what the square on the wall contained. Was it something relative to the murders? Was it a hiding place for evidence in connection with the murders? So many question running through Janice's head that she could not provide answers for, except that she was standing close to the wall that contained the square that Jeff Eldon talked about many times.

Mrs. Walker thought the whole search was a "foolish waste of time" and that it was nothing more than a drunken college kid's imagination. She wondered why anyone would put anything of value, assuming there was something of value hidden within, into an unsecure hole in the wall covered by a piece of that wall. Mrs. Walker was making her thoughts known to everyone when her husband walked into the room with his iPad in hand. Mr. Walker recognized Janice Wilkins from their meeting at the hospital dedication ceremony, and the brief encounter yesterday, after his discharge from the hospital.

Mr. Walker used his iPad to type a message saying "Hi, nice seeing you again" and showed it to Janice. She smiled back at Mr. Walker and asked Mrs. Walker how he is doing. Mr. Walker typed a reply on the iPad which said "I'm much better, T.U. Wud love to B able to talk. Will come sum day. But not soon enuf." Mr. Walker had adapted the iPad to his needs and was using it profusely to communicate when he needed to, or, wanted to.

Mrs. Walker took some time to tell her husband what the group was doing. Mr. Walker listened and then began typing on his iPad. He asked the inevitable question of "why?" Then he wanted to know who had the idea to do this crazy thing? What was found? Then he typed some remarks which seem to question everyone's sanity before he asked his wife where the mystery item was located.

Mrs. Walker told her husband they had not found anything because they were not able to locate the exact location on the living room wall. He type on his iPad, questioning whether, or not, they had referred to some of the photos that were taken by Stephanie and Derek before they had the contractor start his work; something that no one else had remembered.

As Stephanie and Mrs. Walker looked at each other with surprised looks on their faces, Janice Wilkins asked if they could find any of those photos to see if they could help locate the mystery 'square' on the wall. In the meantime Eli and Derek kept feeling their way up and down the wall without discovering anything.

Stephanie went off to search Derek's office closet, while Derek went off to look through boxes in the garage, and Janice and Eli went outside to make phone calls on their cell phones. Mrs. Walker read all the messages her husband typed on his iPad before taking him back upstairs for his afternoon medications.

Almost an hour later, no photos were found in either location, and as everyone gathered in the family room again, Derek decided to have a quick look in Stephanie's office. He quickly scanned the closet shelves and as he was about to close the door, found a large manila-type office envelope with the string ties tied securely. He opened the envelope and found thirty or forty photos that the contractor had taken after they started the remodel work, and another twenty, or so, photos that he and Stephanie had taken of various rooms.

Derek walked into the family room holding a bunch of the pictures in his hand and telling Stephanie that he found the envelope with all the photos. They went through several before finding three photos that clearly showed the 'squared-off' area on the wall.

As they looked at the various photos, Eli remarked that the area appears to be much larger than he thought it would be, and he could not understand why they were not able to feel something under the vinyl which indicated its' location. Derek agreed and said they would go look again; now that they had better indicators. Derek expected they would find the location sooner.

After moving a few pieces of furniture, some antique lamps of Stephanie's, Eli and Derek set about using four of the photos to determine where the 'square' was at on the wall. First thing Derek realized when they started was that he had gotten a really quality job from the contractor that did their remodeling. Both men very slowly felt along the surface of the wall expecting to find something right away, but the contractor had done extensive sanding, and filling in gaps. Neither man could determine a location.

Derek looked at Eli and scratched his head saying, "we may have to cut some of the vinyl wall covering away to find the exact location."

"No, you don't!" exclaimed Stephanie. "We didn't pay all this money for this remodeling to have you simply cut the wall covering away. There must be some other way. Call the contractor and see if they have any recollection of seeing some sort of panel on this wall. What do we find when we find this panel, anyway? Why are we going through all of this? Why decide to destroy a beautiful wall when we don't even know what we are apt to find? " Stephanie suddenly looked as if she had grown two feet taller as she started asking all her questions. She stood with her arms folded across her chest, staring at Derek. Derek knew that posture and look having seen his wife in action in court many times; Stephanie was now on the attack. The best defense? Get answers to her questions.

Derek thought for a second before saying, "you are right. Let me find the phone number for that contractor and give him a phone call to see what he might remember. If nothing else, I can email him a copy of our photos to stimulate his memory. We'll do that before we destroy anything." With that, Derek walked out of the room and into his office to search for a business card.

Mrs. Walker had walked back into the room as Derek exited and asked if anyone wanted to join her for tea.

Stephanie said she would join her mother for tea but Janice Wilkins and Eli said that they had to leave. Janice said that they had other leads and contacts that they needed to follow up on and that it could be some time before Stephanie and Derek knew anything here. She asked Stephanie if she would give her a call when they found something; IF, they found something.

Just as Janice and Eli were saying their 'goodbyes' to Stephanie and Mrs. Walker, Derek walked into the foyer holding his hand up as if to say 'stop!' He continued talking on the phone for another few seconds before saying "thank you. I appreciate your help, very much."

"Well, that was the project foreman who managed our remodel, and he said that they found an old metal box inside an opening in the wall. Unsure what to do with it since it required two oddly shaped keys to open, they put it into a carton of things that went out to the garage for storing. He said he thought that he mentioned it in an email that was sent to me. Now, I received a lot of emails from that company, but I don't remember one that referenced a metal box of any type. It could have been, but I sure don't remember it. Anyway, that carton is now in the boat storage house waiting for a charity to pick it up for a donation."

Stephanie immediately asked if they could go to the boat house and check the carton for the metal box to see if it is still there.

"And, if it is still there, what have you found?" asked Mrs. Walker.

"Mother, we won't know until we get the box opened and see what, if anything, it contains," Stephanie replied. "But we need to find out. There may be nothing, there may be a clue to what happened; maybe who committed the murders."

Janice and Eli asked if they could walk to the boat house with them and see if the metal box contained anything of importance regarding either Keeper House, or the Keeper family murders. Mrs. Walker said she would check on her husband as the others walked down the walkway to the boat house.

Unlocking the door, Derek walked in and turned on a light so they could see. A quick check of three cardboard cartons sitting at the back of the shed quickly exposed a lot of items to be donated to the yacht club's charity drive, and, one large metal box.

The box was fairly heavy as Derek and Eli lifted it out of the carton and set it on a bench along one wall. The box was unlike any that anyone had ever seen before; a brass-like metal with very heavy hinges on the rear. The box was about eight inches tall, and about twenty inches square. On the front were two strange looking locks which would require a key shaped like an inverted 'Y'. A key that everyone admitted they did not remember seeing before. Derek took some tools from the bench and tried to force the cover open without success. He then tampered with the rear hinges in hopes that he could force it open there; no luck. Whoever designed and built this metal box did so with a certainty that it would not be opened by any means other than with its' key, or keys. Eli suggested the possibility of two keys being needed after studying the locks more closely. He showed everyone how one locking mechanism was slightly different from the other in size and in design.

Two keys, it is!

Stephanie stood staring at the box without saying a word. She seemed to almost be staring right through the box without so much as blinking an eye. After a minute, or so, she looked at Derek and asked him if the box was real heavy, or not.

"It's a pretty heavy box," Derek answered. "It's metal, and it's a pretty substantial gauge of metal. Why do you ask?"

Stephanie walked closer to the box as it sat on the bench before looking at Derek. "If you pick it up and shake it can you tell if there's anything inside? Or, no."

Derek looked at Stephanie, picked up the metal box, and tried to shake it vigorously without much success. He then asked Eli to pick one end up while he picked up the other and the two of them would shake it harder.

Even having the two men shake the metal box did not disclose whether, or not, it contained anything inside. The box seemed destined to hold its' secret within, and without the keys to open it would forever stay simply a locked metal box.

Derek decided he would put the metal box into his safe for protection. He asked Janice Wilkins if she had any thoughts on where they might find the keys to unlock it. Janice said that she might have seen a similar key some time ago, but could not remember where, or who had it. She thought it could have been at the hospital dedication ceremony, but was not certain.

Janice Wilkins said she would be continuing her investigation, and her research, on the Keeper House events, and the murder of the members of the Keeper family. She would let Stephanie and Derek know if she discovered anything new. Janice and Eli thanked everyone for their courtesies and hospitalities as they gathered the last of their equipment and left the Victorian.

CHAPTER 14

Dreams. Dreams are sometimes our journey away from reality; away from the real world and into a wondrous world of fantasy and make believe. Unicorns, rainbows, sexually stimulating images and ideas, gently falling rain and the smell of freshly-mown grass to excite our senses. Floating among puffy white clouds as if we are able to fly, and feeling so light that we may never come down to earth.

Dreams that allow us this method of escape are sometimes shattered by thoughts of reality; reality of the worst kind. Reality of fears, of pain, of dark and angry days and nights. Reality that brings us to the brink of torture, and then, once again, sends us back into our feelings of pleasure and bliss. Reality. There is a fine line between reality and make believe; a line so fine as to be non-distinguishable in a dream.

But wait! Is this pain that Tom now feels reality, or is he simply dreaming about it? He feels, he thinks, a sharp dagger-like object poke him in his left side and that feeling is followed by the wet, warm sensation of liquid moving down the skin. Is he dreaming? Is he really feeling something, maybe a knife blade, stick him? There it is again, and again. He must be dreaming, but why does he have to dream about this? Why can't he go back to the dream about the beautiful, naked body he remembers?

Tom feels more, and more, pain as his body receives

more and more stabbings from something very sharp. He longs for a better dream to start but can only feel the pain. Pain traveling from his left side now over to his right, now over to his chest. And the whole time he senses that he is being bathed in a warm liquid as if laying in a tub of tepid water.

The pain seemed to increase, and increase, and last forever. The pain lasted so long that Tom was happy when he went into a big, completely black box in his mind and stopped dreaming. Nothing. No pain. No dreaming. Just absolute and complete blackness.

Tom did not know how long he laid in the absolute blackness. He did not know of any dreams, good or bad. He did not know about any pain; pain which seemed to leave him completely without feelings.

He only knew about the huge, blindingly bright light that he saw when he looked at the ceiling. A light so bright that he could not continue looking at it and had to close his eyes, once again. Was he dreaming again? Was he outside looking up at the sun? He could not answer any of these questions.

Tom seemed to drift in and out of sleep and remembered hearing voices every once and awhile. He finally heard someone's voice saying his name and this startled him. He could not open his eyes long because of the light which kept blinding him. Tom finally turned his head slightly to his right and opened his eyes to see three very unclear figures standing close by him. He could not make out who they were but he knew they were talking about him, and were close.

Tom tried to get some moisture in his mouth and throat so that he could speak. No luck. Both mouth and throat were dryer than a patch of desert real estate. He tried to move his arms and hands to motion to the people near by that he needed some water. Again, no luck. Tom was not able to move either arm, or hands. Something has them anchored down, fastened to the surface he laid on.

Finally, Tom barked out the sound of "bokker." This sound seemed to startle the three people and ended their conversation. Tom knew that he had said "water", but the group heard Tom bark out "bokkah."

Tom continued to try to focus the people into clarity so he would know where he was at. It wasn't happening quickly. He was able to see that one person was wearing what appeared to be a nurses uniform. This, he could not make sense of because he was certain that he was still dreaming.

"By deer, midder bitchen," she said as she felt his wrist for a pulse.

"Wop?" Tom mumbled. Tom began to feel that words were not being spoken clearly, and did not know why. He strained to focus the person into clarity and ask more questions. It seemed to take a long time before he could see the nurse taking his heart rate clearly. He could discern what she was doing, he just could not hear her speak clearly.

Finally, another nurse gave Tom a glass of water with a straw in it for him to sip with. Tom did not hesitate when he started drinking the liquid. He drank the entire contents of the glass and felt like his throat might begin to work properly after a short coughing spell. He swallowed hard, and tried to speak.

"Could I have more, please?" Tom asked the nurse as she moved the empty glass away. "I am very thirsty."

"Of course, Mr. Kitchen," she replied.

The other nurse asked Tom if he could hear her now, to which Tom replied that he could. "Before," Tom told her, "I could not understand words I heard. Everything was garbled. Nothing made sense."

The nurse smiled and told Tom that he responded to her when she earlier said "Hi, there Mr. Kitchen." She asked if those words were garbled, or not. Tom told her that what he heard was completely different than what she just said.

As the second nurse returned with a second glass of water for Tom, he asked "where am I, and what is going on with me?"

As Tom sipped more water from the glass, the first nurse told him that he had been brought in by ambulance from his home after a news reporter called 9-1-1 saying that she had found him laying on a couch in a pool of blood with many stab wounds. That was three days ago, and they have been trying to keep him alive ever since. The ER doctors had to perform two operations on him already, and he has been recovering since the second operation was concluded.

Tom asked why his arms and hand were tied down and unable to be moved. The nurse said that was a precaution against Tom reacting violently in his sleep and trying to pull his IV's out of his arms. She said that after the doctor examines Tom, that he may have them removed; but that is the doctor's decision to make.

The nurses continued with their tasks in Tom's room and made copious notes on his charts before they both left. Now Tom was really curious as to what had happened to him, who is responsible, and of course: Why? He laid in his hospital bed unable to move very much, and thought about the dreams that he thought he had had.

Why did he dream about clouds, flowing rivers, and a naked woman? Why, indeed. He tried to link various subjects together to make sense of something, but was not able to. He thought about many things, and listened to the sounds coming from the hallway outside his room until he fell asleep.

It seemed like a peaceful sleep of only a few minutes and Tom was amazed when he determined from the clock on the wall of his room that he had been asleep over four hours. A nurse was asking him if he was hungry, or not, and wanted dinner brought in. Tom asked who would feed it to him as his hands and arms were still tied down with restraints. The nurse simply smiled as she turned to leave the room nearly bumping into Dr. Chambers as he entered Tom's room.

"Well, it's good to see you with your eyes opened. How is your pain level, on a scale of one to ten?" Dr. Chambers asked as he read Tom's charts and looked at the monitors connected to him.

"Good to see you, too, doctor. I guess my pain level is right about a seven plus. Maybe an eight." Tom replied as he looked around the room. "When can I get some movement in my arms and hands? I'd like to be able to scratch my nose, if it itches, as well as feed myself. Understand that most other things are being done for me."

The doctor smiled at Tom replying "I don't see any reason why we can't remove the restraints now, as long as you promise not to remove any sensors or any thing else from your body. This is much more serious than your malaria illness was; this nearly cost you your life. You were attacked quite severely and stabbed eleven times. Five of those stab wounds were major incisions and caused major trauma to you. We had to perform two major operating procedures to save your life, so we can't have any more set backs. You need to heal completely. You are becoming a regular in this hospital and I think you would like to spend time elsewhere for a while. Am I correct?"

"Yes, you are," Tom responded, "and I have a lot of work that needs to get done. How long do you think I will be here, this time, doctor?"

Dr. Chambers explained in more graphic details the healing process that Tom would need as he removed the arm and hand restraints. He was listening to Tom's heart and breathing when two men walked into the room and identified themselves as police detectives who were there to ask Tom some questions about his assault.

Dr. Chambers asked Tom how he was feeling and if he was able to answer some questions from the detectives. Tom looked at the two police detectives and said that he would try, but he did not remember much of what had happened to him.

Dr. Chambers told the detectives that he would stay and monitor Tom's vitals and would have to stop the Q&A session if his patient's vitals did not stay within an acceptable range. The detectives agreed and started asking the obvious questions about who did Tom think would want to do this to him and why. Tom did not have any idea. Has Tom had any arguments or altercations with someone recently who might want to see him dead? Tom has no recollection of any arguments, or disagreements, and certainly no fights with anyone. One detective said that since Tom owned many local companies, could he have made some competitor of one of his businesses mad enough to want to kill him? Tom said that he did not have any major competitors, other than two jewelry stores that catered to an entirely different type of customer base, so there was no one that he knew of that would do something like this.

One of the detectives asked Tom what he remembered about the assault, to which Tom replied "nothing, really." Tom went on to explain that he had gotten out of the hospital, had gone to each of his businesses to see what had been going on. He spent some time at his Ace Hardware store going over items with his manager; started feeling feverish and ill, again, and left to go home to rest and medicate. Not feeling better when he got home, he quickly took his quinine and doxycycline tablets and some aspirins before getting into bed to rest.

One detective then asked if Tom remembered hearing any noises around his house, or what he heard when he awoke.

Tom then tried to explain that he went to sleep. Sound,

didn't-hear-a-damn-thing-asleep. Only dreams; really weird, unusual dreams until he woke up in the hospital room.

Dr. Chambers asked Tom if he remembered anything about the dream he had. Tom answered that it was a series of dreams, and that they were each very, very strange. Like he was floating among clouds in one, bathing in a warm liquid in another, and repeated, painful stabbing-like feelings that never seem to stop or go away.

After Dr. Chambers asked a few more questions of Tom, he excused himself and went to a computer terminal at the nurses station while the two PD detectives continued with their list of questions.

One detective asked Tom where he contracted malaria from, to which Tom replied that he got it in Central America years ago when he was working with the Peace Corps while in college. Tom told him that he had only had one flare-up of malaria since then. The two detectives continued asking Tom questions, most of which he was unable to answer. When it appeared that they were about to conclude their questioning session with Tom, Dr. Chambers walked back into the room.

"Tom, I just checked the lab report of your blood workup and found substantial quantities of a substance that is a slow-working, sleep-inducing drug which is only found in a very small region of the world." Dr. Chambers told Tom. "Do you remember eating anything, or drinking any liquid before you returned home?"

Tom thought for a couple minutes before answering "no." He related how he started feeling bad while talking with his manager at the hardware store, gathered up some financial papers to take home and review, and left the store.

Dr. Chambers asked Tom about how long after he got home did he fall asleep, to which Tom told the doctor that it was not more than fifteen to twenty minutes. Tom got home, thought about eating something, but did not, drank some water, felt like his fever was increasing, and went to bed. Dr. Chambers looked at Tom for a few seconds and asked him if he had ever used cocaine, or any similar drug. Tom said "no!" The doctor continued to ask Tom more questions before Tom interrupted him saying "something unusual happened as I left the store. Unusual in the sense that I barely recalled it, but, as I went to leave the store, we were getting a delivery at the back door; a big delivery of several pallet loads of merchandise. Seeing this, I decided to turn around and go out the front door. As I turned, the driver of the delivery truck stumbled and fell onto me, knocking me to the floor. As I went to get up, I felt a slight pain in my right buttock, but did not think about it as I was more mad at the bumbling fool who had just knocked me down. He apologized profusely in his broken English, but I never stopped to check out my butt."

With that, Dr. Chambers asked Tom if he could have a quick look. Tom agreed and pulled back the sheets for the doctor to look at his right butt cheek. After seeing a small red mark on Tom's 'glut', Dr. Chambers calls for a nurse to bring him a sample kit so that he can swab the area and send it to the laboratory for analysis.

In the meantime, one of the police detectives asked Tom for as much of a description of the delivery man that Tom could recall. Tom thought for a few seconds before starting his description of the Latino man with a scruffy beard and a neck tattoo of some sort. The more that Tom described the man, the more the two detectives looked at each other with puzzled looks upon their faces. After a few minutes, the second police detective interrupted Tom and asked him to look at a picture that he had on his cell phone.

The man pictured on the officer's phone was very similar to the man who knocked Tom down in his store, but not an exact match. "Don't think that he's the guy," Tom told the officer. "The guy who knocked me down had shorter hair and more graying around the temples than that fellow shows."

The officer then showed Tom another picture of the same man except this photo concentrated on his neck tattoo which was some sort of bird flying through a ring of vines, and had a sun behind both objects. Tom looked at the photo and looked at the detective showing it to him.

"I've seen that tattoo before, somewhere." Tom told him. "I can't remember where, exactly, but I know I've seen it before."

The officer went on to tell Tom that this is one of many members of the Mendoza family that are being investigated by police departments in Boston, New York City, and in Hartford. "They are believed to have become a gang of murderers, thieves and drug peddlers that have moved into neighborhoods in various cities and replaced existing gangs by whatever means necessary. They are tough, they are mean, and they are deadly to anyone NOT a family member. With a very large male base, they started branching out into areas as the family brought more cousins, nephews, and, now even have some female members of the gang doing business in New York. The NYPD arrested several gang members for suspicion of murder and extortion a couple months ago. They were granted bail by a judge suspected of being on their payroll, and have not been seen since. They apparently left the country for either Mexico or Central America somewhere."

The detective explained that the neck tattoo that all members of the Mendoza mob have is part of their acceptance into the 'family'. After passing some sort of secret initiation, they are taken to a family member who imparts the family creed to them, and then they are given a neck tattoo as a final showing of acceptance. The detective went on to say that it was always believed that the head of the family was Jesus Mendoza and that he did the tattooing on new members, but Jesus had disappeared a while ago and has not been seen since.

Tom listened to everything the detective was telling him as if each word was brand new and unknown to him. He knew about Jesus Mendoza; he knew when he disappeared and how. Tom knew that Jesus would never be doing another tattoo on a new gang member. Tom knew a lot more than he really cared to know. He listened to the detective and tried to form some questions to ask that would not sound like he knew anything at all.

As the detective continued telling Tom about the Mendoza Mob, Tom asked a couple questions as Dr. Chambers came back into the room with a handful of papers. He looked at the two police detectives, then at Tom and said "the lab tests prove it! The delivery guy, or someone else, injected you with a very powerful, hallucinogenic drug that took somewhere between twenty and forty-five minutes to completely knock you out. While you were knocked out you probably were experiencing the actual attack, complete with the painful part of it, and your brain told you that you were dreaming. What he gave you was very, very strong and could have been fatal if you had gotten a few more 'cc's.'"

The detective asked if he could see the lab report that Dr. Chambers held so that he could get the correct spelling of the drugs.

When Dr. Chambers had to respond to a page, the two police detectives thanked both Tom and the doctor for their time and cooperation and said that they would be in touch if they had more questions. They left to continue their investigation over at the Ace Hardware store.

With the room empty, Tom relaxed and tried to compose a clearer picture of the fellow who knocked him over at the hardware store. He remembered looking at the man, his clothes, his every feature and not seeing anything unusual or memorable about him other than being Latino. Tom thought about that occurrence so much that it put him into a sound sleep. A deep sleep, this time, without dreams or pain.

CHAPTER 15

The day was, as someone once said, a "real Chamber of Commerce" type of day. Moderate temperatures, blue skies spotted with small, puffy, white clouds, and a gentle breeze so soft that it barely moved hair on your head. The type of day that everyone, and anyone, who lived in 'snow country' during the winter, would gladly welcome many more of. The type of day that Janice Wilkins did not want to spend indoors going through dusty, old County Recorder records; but she knew she had to. Like it or not.

The County Recorders office had started to digitize all their old records many years ago, but it was a very long, time-consuming, process that an office, that is very under staffed, could not devote full time and efforts to. Janice knew she would have to do some 'digging' if she hoped to find the information that she sought. She had the tract, grid, and lot information from previous researches so she would save some time there.

Janice found a large, unused, table where she could spread out her iPhone, micro recorder and notebooks in case she found something in her searching. She started going through the digitized records first; tons of information concerning property she was not interested in, people she didn't know, or want to know about, and transfers, sales, and improvements on everything except the Keeper House Victorian. She completed her examination of all the digital records before starting on the books, and books of information not yet digitized. She covered years going back into the twentieth century and finally started finding references to Keeper House that she sought. Page after page of construction permits, remodeling permits, land sale notices, land modification permits, and other miscellaneous copies pertaining to the Victorian.

Janice was nearing exhaustion, and boredom, and not finding anything that she thought was valuable pertaining to the Victorian when she found an old permit titled "Special Application for Title Transfer". She read it twice trying to understand what exactly it covered, but only extracted a couple names, a date, and dates that the application was submitted and approved. She did note a reference made to being witnessed by the managing editor, and a co-owner of the Westport News newspaper. Janice wondered why outside, non-county government, people would be involved in witnessing a 'Special Application'. She wondered why but never found any clues within the pages of the books she examined.

Janice made copious notes, recordings, and took pictures of what she found, whether she understood what it was or not, her experience told her to have copies of it even though the elderly woman who showed her to her work area reminded her that photographing county records was not allowed. Janice's next stop would be the offices of the Westport News newspaper to see what sort of records they kept.

The 'News' had once been a daily newspaper with wide distribution, but, as many other print papers had come to realize, the reading of a daily print paper was not practiced by many people and so it had to become a weekly print, or disappear completely.

Janice introduced herself to the manager in the office, and told him what she would like to do. He listened intently and said that she could search any records still kept there, but she would have to do her research tomorrow morning as it was ten minutes past closing and he was just heading out the door.

"Ten minutes past closing time?" Janice thought to herself, you are supposed to be a news person, and should be more concerned about what you can do to provide for your readers, and not about closing time. Janice knew that this was not a battle she wanted to start, nor would it be a battle she would win, so she smiled and thank the man and asked what time the office would open in the morning. With that information filed away, Janice left and headed for her car and her highway home; her research and the unanswered questions would wait.

Janice reviewed her notes and pictures that night trying to understand what everything referred to before having some wine with her light dinner and heading off to bed. Her husband had left earlier in the day for a four day real estate conference and continuing education sessions, so Janice has the entire house to herself tonight. An unusual occurrence.

The following morning Janice arrived at the newspaper office fifteen minutes early, only to have to wait until twenty past the hour. Seems small town news people do not have to keep the same schedule as news people in major cities do. When the manager arrived he apologized for being late saying that he had to cover a local fire about two hours earlier and it lasted longer than expected. Janice simply said that she understood and would like to get started with her research if there was a place where she could spread things out a little.

The manager showed Janice to a small side storage room where she was given the use of a small table that was about the size of a card table, and, about as sturdy as one, also. She looked at the stacks, and stacks of old boxes, newspapers and miscellaneous junk, and thanked the man as he turned to leave saying that he has work to do back in the 'layout room.' Janice thanked him, again, and started to look through the master file of newspapers.

Two and a half hours later Janice found a reference to the murders of the Keeper family that pointed to an earlier issue for more details. She read the article along with several others before going onto other issues of the paper, making notes as she went. Finally, she found the paper from the morning after the murders happened which seemed to cover everything in great detail. It contained a photo showing five bodies covered by tarps, and a large, dark, stain on the wooden flooring. The article went into naming all four of the Keeper children and giving their ages, as well as naming both parents and telling how successful Mr. Keeper had been as a businessman. The story went on to tell about how police were baffled as to who committed the crime, and how the local police department, who were understaffed and lack any type of technology, asked for help from the F.B.I. in solving the murders. Janice read the complete story twice and studied the black and white photo of the murder scene which, for some unknown reason, bothered her. She looked at the photo and studied it more, and more before realizing that the number of bodies on the floor didn't match with the number of people listed. Two parents and four children of the Keeper family equaled six victims. In the photo were clearly seven tarps covering dead bodies. Janice studied the photo for several minutes before seeing that the photo was credited to a journalist/photographer named Lola McBride from the Hartford Courant newspaper.

This information caught Janice by surprise, as she had met a Lola McBride at Yale University, while doing a story for CNN. While Lola was a professor of eastern European History, and Janice's investigation was into alleged sporting events score fixing, Janice knew of Lola through one of her sorority sisters, Lara Ireland. Lara and Janice not only belong to the same sorority, but had taken several classes together and pulled many 'all-nighters' together with other sorority sisters before finals.

Janice knew that Lara Ireland had gone to work for the federal government in the State Department, and was working somewhere outside the country currently. She thought, for half-a-second, about trying to contact her, but quickly gave up on that thought in favor of calling Yale and seeing if she could reach Lola McBride. Her hopes were that, if she talked to Lola, that her memory of that event would be good enough to confirm, or correct, Janice's body counts. Janice decided that this was the perfect time to take a break from newspapers and picked up her iPhone to search for phone numbers.

Janice's mother used to tell her that "sometimes, it's better to be lucky than good." She always remembered that when good luck would find her, and this appeared to be another one of those times. After only about five, to six, minutes of calling, introducing herself as being with CNN, asking a question, or two, Janice got to the office for Professor Lola McBride.

Janice began with what she thought would be a lengthy story of why she was calling, and who she is, only to be surprised by Lola's quick, and joyous greeting of "well, hi there young lady. I haven't talked to you since graduation day at college. Wait! Maybe, two years after that weren't you and Lara both at the sorority's spring get-together in Boston?"

Janice was already amazed at Lola's recollection of times and events, even before she had much of a chance to speak.

"Professor McBride, you're fabulous! I had all but forgotten about that spring get-together in Boston until now. How is Lara doing?" Janice asked.

Lola laughed lightly and replied that "Lara is doing great. She's with the State Department working in Mumbai, India, got married, as you know, and her husband is teaching advance electronics and technology at Mumbai's 'Indian Institute of Technology Bombay'. They have three children and have adjusted to living in the Indian way of life. We all missed seeing you at their wedding, Janice. It was a grand event."

"So I heard from some of our 'sisters'. Wanted to be there, but I was in Jail when they got married. Not for anything that I had done, just for being in the wrong place at the wrong time while doing my job." Janice said. "Well, I am so glad to hear they are doing well. Do you think they will stay in India forever, or, possibly return to the U.S. one day?"

"I'm not sure, but Lara has hinted that she may be reassigned one day. Won't say where, although she is brushing up on her French a lot." Lola responded. "But, Janice I'm not feeling that this is why you phoned me, and, I have another class in twenty minutes. What can I do for you?"

Janice Wilkins went on to explain what she was investigating, why she was investigating it, and her questions regarding a photo in the newspaper credited to Lola as photographer and reporter. She asked Lola if she did, in fact, take the photo, and what she remembered of the murder scene.

Lola confirmed that she did take the photo, only because she was the only reporter who knew how to operate a brand new Nikon camera given to the newspaper. She, and a male reporter were sent to Yale University to try and photograph a sporting event between Yale and UCONN, the University of Connecticut. When their assignment was over, Lola asked her male driver to drive down to Westport to see an ailing aunt, and while driving to the aunt's house, which was only a few blocks away from the Keeper House mansion, they heard about the murders. Lola phoned her editor to get permission to stay and cover the murders, to which he agreed but only because it involved the Keeper family.

Janice questioned Lola about what her photo showed for body count and what the various news stories reported.

Lola explained that, at the time this happened, she was not yet twenty-three years old and this was a major traumatic event for her. She had completed her undergrad studies in Journalism, and History, and was working at the newspaper while completing grad studies in History. She, as she already admitted, was sent on this assignment to Yale because she could operate the brand new Nikon camera equipment without braking it. When she and her reporter with her walked into the living room of the mansion, she nearly gagged and lost her lunch.

The police were scurrying to get tarps and cover the bodies before anyone saw them, but Lola and her reporter were too fast for them. She remembered having to go back outside to get some deep breaths while her reporter got some information about the deceased from a police sergeant. When she had composed herself, she took her camera and went to work shooting photos of everything that she could. She remembered thinking that the police were either going to stop her at any second, or to demand she turn over her camera and film to them; time was of the essence.

Lola paused for a moment, as if to compose herself after recalling the murder scene, before focusing on the scene in her mind. She softly started recalling the bodies, whether they were male or female, child or adult, and exactly where they were laying in the room. She remembered how some of the local police were walking through the various pools of blood without regard to what it was, nor what they were doing to a crime scene.

Suddenly Lola stopped her recollections and paused for several seconds before telling Janice that Janice was correct. "There were the four Keeper children laying about the living room in different locations, there was both Mr. and Mrs. Keeper laying about three feet apart, AND, there was a dark hair young man, or maybe even a teenager, laying in a smaller pool of blood back behind a large wing-back chair. I remember him because he was away from the rest of the family members, and he was clasping an odd shaped key in his right hand. A key that looked like an inverted 'Y' at one end, and I had never seen anything like that before. Since then I have seen similar shaped keys in history books, but that was my first time. Now, if we count all those dead bodies, I believe we come up with a total of seven. Not six. Do you agree?"

Janice agreed. The total is seven and as she looked at the photo again, the angle that the photo was shot from showed only a foot protruding out from under a tarp behind a large chair. She asked Lola if anyone ever found out who the 'extra' victim was, and why he was killed also. Lola said she did not know, that she and her reporter only stayed over night at her Aunt's house and were barred from the Victorian the following morning.

When Lola and her reporter returned to the

newspaper's offices, all her photos and notes were turned over to another team of reporters without reason or explanation. Lola admitted that she felt a bit angry about that happening, as though she had done something wrong. But the editor's decision is law! Lola and her reporter were each given new, and separate assignments, and Lola went on to complete her graduate studies and leave the newspaper business.

Lola stopped talking and was quiet for a few seconds before saying "you might find out more information if you can locate a fellow named Albert Franklin, or a Ben Jessup. They were the two men assigned to follow up on the murders and write the story. I believe it might even be Ben Jessup's name on the article. I hate to end this on that note, but I have to go teach some 'eager-to-learn' young men and women about a certain Peloponnesian War. Write down my cell phone number and call me any time, but for now I must go."

Janice thanked Lola profusely and said that she had been a tremendous help to her and her investigation into the Keeper murders. Janice wished her a good day and said she would phone her occasionally to see how things were going, and would not stay out of touch this long ever again.

With that, the phone call ended and Janice went back to reading all the articles about the murders that she could locate. She gave thought to driving up to Hartford and reviewing their newspapers, also, but that would have to wait for another day. While she was talking with Lola McBride, Janice's assignment editor sent her a new assignment which would take her to Providence, Rhode Island for a while.

Before Janice left the small room she took pictures of all her notes, some stories from various issues of the local newspaper, and a couple photos of the picture in the newspaper of the murder scene. When done she went to find the manager to thank him and ask him if she could clean up and put thing away for him.

Janice finally found him in the rear of the building, well beyond the old printing presses, movable drawers of type, and many other reminders of the printing business from many years ago. He was in a large, very well lighted room which said "Layout Room" on the glass door. He asked if she was leaving and Janice said 'yes' before thanking him and asking about cleaning up the room she had used.

Before he could answer Janice, a very large man came through a doorway at the other end of the room. He was dressed in a black, pin-striped, suit with a violet shirt with a black/gray/violet striped tie. At first glance Janice thought he had just stepped out of a movie about gangsters from the thirties or forties. He did not smile when he introduced himself as "Gabriel Franklin. But, just call me Gabe." Seems Mr. Franklin is one of the new owners of the

KEEPER OF THE KEY

Westport newspaper and wanted to help Janice with whatever she needed from it.

Janice said she was glad to meet him but that she had to leave as her boss just gave her a new assignment down the road in Stamford and she had to meet her cameraman who is outside waiting.

Gabe smile slightly and said that "sounds interesting. Trading Westport for Stamford. Something big? Must be something big to dispatch a CNN reporter and cameraman to Stamford. How big a story is it?"

Janice was now getting a little uneasy at Gabe's questioning and decided not to expand her lie any more. She said she would find out on her way there as she was waiting for a call from her editor. She thanked both men, again, for their allowing her to research back issues of the newspaper, and wished them both a good day.

Janice turned to head back through the big warehouse to the front door when Gabe said "you drive carefully. There are some wild, crazy drivers out there on our roads and you can never tell what might happen, Ms. Wilkins. Never can tell. Oh, and hope you had a nice talk with Lola McBride."

Janice now had goose bumps on top of goose bumps and chills running from the nape of her neck, all the way down her spine. She hesitated half a second but did not turn around or respond to Gabe's remarks.

CHAPTER 16

Tom enjoyed the sunshine and the warmth spreading across his face so much that he decided he did not want to ever go back into a hospital. He sat and watched people walk to and fro, watched dog walkers doing their jobs with good groupings of canines, and some not-so-good groupings. He wished that there was a park close by the hospital so he could spend the rest of today on a bench just 'people watching', and being amazed at how much energy small children have. Children always amazed Tom, in oh-so-many ways, and he could sit and watch them run and play for hours. He would love to be able to do that, but his taxi was just turning into the hospital driveway to come take him home.

While everything was nearly perfect with Tom's healing, he still could not drive a car until the police department checked him out and signed off on his ability to operate a vehicle.

The nurse wheeled Tom to the back door of his taxi and gave the driver a note with Tom's address on it. She also gave the driver instructions that they were not to stop anywhere except for Tom's house; no matter what Tom said. She then told him to bill the hospital for fees and tips as the passenger did not have any money on him. With that, she bid Tom farewell and reminded Tom of his next, follow-up, doctors appointment. She closed the rear door and watched as the taxi pulled away and headed for the driveway's exit.

As Tom rode along inside the taxi, he remembered all the things that had happened to him over the last several months. Episodes with his brother, George, the untimely death of his younger sister, Sally, health episodes for himself, and the seemingly-abrupt disappearance of his older sister, Helen. He didn't know if he should feel grateful or be nervous about what might be coming next.

As the taxi got near his home, Tom saw a car parked in his driveway that he did not recognize. He really didn't want company today, so he wondered how he would get rid of whomever it was. As the taxi pulled into the driveway, Tom saw the manager from his Ace Hardware store get out of the parked auto and come back toward Tom's taxi. Tom thanked the driver and slowly got out of the rear seat to shake the hand of his manager.

Tom's manager first apologized for being there when Tom got home. He said that he was writing a note to Tom, when he saw the taxi pull in the driveway behind him. He was leaving Tom some sales figures, some checks that only Tom could sign, and a small bag full of Tom's mail. Tom thanked him and asked if he wanted to come in for a drink, to which he thanked Tom and declined saying he had to get to his son's T-ball practice. Tom asked him to put everything on a table just inside the front door as he unlocked the door to his house.

After his manager left, Tom sat down in his favorite living room chair with the bag of mail and folder of items that had been left for him. He listened to the quiet of his house and welcomed it after hearing nothing but noise while in the hospital. Tom listened to the quiet for several minutes before falling asleep.

When Tom awoke he was both hungry and bewildered. Bewildered because he was not aware of where he was at for several seconds, and hungry because he had missed dinner at the hospital due to his early departure. He finally realized, after nearly a minute, that he was at home, and he had better find something for himself to eat. He made his way out to his kitchen and started preparing some unspoiled food that he found in his refrigerator. Tom figured that something eatable was better than hunger. He made a mental note to go food shopping tomorrow; a note quickly erased when he realized that he could not, yet, drive his car. Once again, he would have to rely on other people for help.

Tom had to admit, at least to himself if not to anyone else, that as good as the food at the hospital was, his cooking was much better tonight. He enjoyed being by himself, leisurely eating dinner and watching the late night variety shows on cable. He told himself that as good as he felt, he would feel even better tomorrow morning after another nights' sleep.

The morning brought some glorious sunshine, warm temperatures, blue sky and about three puffy white clouds. Tom stood at his bedroom window just taking every bit of it in and being very thankful to be at home. He watched the little birds fly around, avoiding each other and seeming to play some sort of 'dodging' game with one another. After about fifteen minutes of watching and breathing in the fresh, clean morning air, Tom decided to see if he could scrounge together something for his breakfast.

Scrambled eggs, a couple Trader Joe's hash brown potato patties, and some very strong coffee down the throat and suddenly Tom was a new man. He cleaned up his kitchen and decided to start going through his bundles of mail and papers that his manager had brought him from the hardware store. He cleared off his dining room table to use the large surface to sort through all the mail, and such.

Tom had completed one and a half shopping bags full of advertisements, surveys, 'vote-for-me' political mailers and various other pieces when he noticed two manila-type mailing envelopes amongst the others. Both a very large envelope, and a slightly smaller one, were without postage, a return address, or a completed address for Tom. Both had been handwritten with only Tom's name, but each in a different hand writing. Tom picked up the smaller of the two envelopes and opened the sealed flap. As he extracted the paper inside, he felt a warm glow come over him because he saw it was a poem handwritten on plain copy paper. He knew immediately who wrote it, and as he read it, he knew that his sister Helen was alive somewhere. It was written in code that the Keeper siblings had set up many years ago. The poem read:

THE FISH DON'T HOLLER,

THE ROCKS DON'T YELL.

I'VE BEEN THRU HEAVEN,

AND, I'M GOING THRU HELL.

I'VE CLIMBED THE MOUNTAIN,

AND I'VE TOUCHED THE CLOUDS,

I'M ONE MINUS ZERO,

SO I'LL SCREAM OUT LOUD.

I'LL NEVER LAUGH, NOR EVER SING,

I'M HEADED FOR AN EAGLE WITHOUT A RING.

Anyone who happened to read this poem would not have a clue as to who wrote it, or what it meant. Code that to Tom told him that Helen has undergone some horrendous event in her life, she is emotionally damaged, but physically okay, and will meet Tom in Manhattan at a certain clothing store on her birthday. Her birthday is still over two weeks away, but Tom was excited to know that she was okay and he would be seeing her soon. He leaned back in his chair and smiled to himself at receiving such good news.

He reached for the larger envelope, which also only had Tom's name hand written on the front of it, opened it and removed a large, ten-by twelve inch, color photo from inside. He dropped the photo on the table as if he had just been severely burned by an extremely hot object and let out a very loud, very long, gut-wrenching scream "nooooooooo!"

He sat staring at the photo laying on top of various pieces of mail, his entire body shaking uncontrollably and not able to believe what his eyes were focused on. He sat shaking and sobbing for two to three minutes before being able to touch the photo, once again, and pick it up for a closer look.

The photo was of a muddy dirt road somewhere, with a bloodied, and very mangled body laying in a large pool of blood. Tire tracks on each side showed that it was probably a rural road and splatters from rain drops could be seen in the many pools of water in those tire tracks. All that Tom could see, though, was the dead body of his brother Gerald. Or, George Kitchen.

As Tom was finally able to study the photo, he saw the shadow of at least five men standing off, behind the camera. He studied the photo in hopes of getting a clue as to who these 'hidden' men might be, but he pretty well knew who they were, already. Tom felt something on the back of the photo and turned it over to find a yellow 'Post-It-Note' attached which read: "His final words were 'don't ever miss another payment to the Nicaraguans again!' There was no name written, but Tom knew that it was Ernesto Siguenya, or one of his men, who was trying to remind Tom of his financial obligations to the Nicaraguan group; something that Tom had been reminded of after his last hospital stay. Since there were no dates on either the photo or the note, Tom could not tell if George had been murdered before, or after, he made the payments to Ernesto's Canadian bank account. Payments made late, but, made.

It took several more minutes before Tom's body stopped shaking from head to toe, and he was able to go to the kitchen to pour himself another cup of coffee. He stood by the kitchen counter thinking about the cruelty of the way that George was murdered. Something to impress Tom with? Or, some way to drive home a point with Tom? Tom picked up the photo, again, and studied every inch of it while sipping his cup of coffee. Finally, he determined that there was nothing visible that could tell him anything about what happened, where it happened, or who the men were that did it. George was gone, and now there was only Tom and his sister Helen.

A knock on the front door brought Tom back to reality. He dropped the photo and both envelopes into a drawer in a living room end table before opening the front door to find his hardware store manager standing there smiling.

"I hope I'm not disturbing you, Mr. Kitchen," he said, "but I know that you're unable to drive yet, so I thought I would stop by and pick up the checks that you signed and take into work with me. If that's okay, that is."

Tom smiled and invited him in. Offering him a cup of coffee Tom told him that he had fallen asleep last night and didn't get the checks signed. "However, if you will have a cup of coffee with me, I can sign them right now and you can take them with you."

Tom's manager agreed and sat down to drink his cup of coffee while Tom read each checks' attachment before signing all of them. He gave them all to his manager, told him that he would not be in the store for a few days and asked if there was anything major coming up. His manager told Tom about a major promotion on paint that was starting week after next, and of a visit from the national Ace Hardware people to Tom's store which is scheduled to happen in about three weeks. Tom told him that he thought he would be there for the visit from the national Ace people, but he would probably not be back before then.

"Back?" asked the manager. "You going on a trip?"

"I have a very sick aunt upstate New York that I'm going to try, and I emphasize TRY, to visit before she passes away. Don't know if I will make it, but I have to try." Tom answered. To anyone else, Tom would not have given any form of explanation, but to his hardware store manager, who had gone well beyond the role of just being an employee, he felt obligated to give some information. Even if it was not the truth.

Tom's manager gathered up all the signed checks and left for the store after asking Tom if there was anything that he could do, or get, for him before he left. Tom thanked him and said "no. I'll be okay once I figure out how to do some grocery shopping without driving my car." The manager offered to go to the market for Tom, but Tom said 'no', saying he had plenty of food, just not things he had a craving for.

Tom's real intention was to wait until close to evening, when the sunlight was beginning to be chased away by darkness, and try to drive his car. First, maybe just around the block, and then maybe tomorrow he would try a little longer effort. He was unsure about the effects of the drugs he was taking, so he didn't want to, no, that's not correct, he did want to but he decided he would not, try to do too much at one time. He went to his kitchen to take inventory of exactly what he had in usable food. He then would check his walk-in pantry and that would determine how long he could hold out before having to venture to the market.

Tom also decided that he would remove the photo and the envelopes, along with the coded message from his sister, from the drawer in the living room, and put them in a locked desk drawer in his home office. He didn't think that someone would come into his house and start going through drawers in his living room, but he wasn't going to take a chance, either. Tom Kitchen had not made it this far by taking unnecessary chances.

Tom's Jeep is certainly not your 'best-friend-let's-go-hunting-or-fishing' type of Jeep; it is a Jeep Commander, the top of the line model with power everything to make driving effortless. So, Tom slowly backed the Jeep out of his garage, onto his driveway, and slowly onto the street. So far, so good. He eased the automatic transmission into 'drive' and slowly the large vehicle moved forward and down Tom's block until he guided it into a right turn.

Eight minutes later, Tom eased the Jeep back into his garage and turned off the engine. "Whew!" he said to himself, feeling like he had completed a major accomplishment. It took another minute of sitting behind the steering wheel before Tom noticed both of his hands and arms, and his right leg, were shaking badly. He figured that this was just from the strain and being nervous that someone would see him, or he would get stopped by a patrol car for something.

Another five minutes and his body had completely calmed down and the shaking had ended, leaving Tom feeling better and ready for tomorrow's longer attempt.

CHAPTER 17

It only took Janice Wilkins three days of probing and questioning in Providence, Rhode Island, to complete her assignment there, and then she was off to Boston for a couple days before heading west and back to Connecticut for more research into Keeper House, and the murders of the Keeper family. By now, both topics were becoming somewhat of an obsession with Janice and she knew she would only be satisfied when all facts were uncovered and known to everyone. Janice's husband had finally learned how to deal with, and be patient with, his wife's obsessions, but only after much frustration on his part.

Janice met her husband-to-be while in college, and Howard Wilkins learned early-on that she could become obsessed with both major things, as well as little things. Little things like having a perfect paper for her professor, or arranging the perfect gathering at her sorority. But after fourteen years of marriage, Howard focused on his real estate business, which had grown quite large and very profitable, and let Janice focus on winning more Peabody Awards, and more Emmys for her CNN specials.

Janice Wilkins had stumbled across something while doing research in Providence that she felt needed further examination. Further examination, though, would require her to go to Hartford and spend time going through the state's records of birth, deaths, and such. She knew the drive from Boston to Hartford would be a test for her, but it had to be made. She thought to herself "thank, God, for audio books and good cell coverage," as she started her drive out of Boston.

Meanwhile, Tom Kitchen was now able to drive his Jeep Commander all around the neighborhood without problems; and, the shaking had stopped in both hands and his leg. He had phoned the police captain in Bridgeport to ask when he could get his license back, but had not gotten a call back, yet. For now, he would have to be patient and settle for his secret practice drives within the neighborhood.

Tom had also sent another coded message to his sister and had not gotten any response from her. He didn't know if she was in New York City, or back home in Bridgeport as she was not at the hospital every time Tom phoned. Getting any further information from anyone there would require Tom divulging his relationship to their Chief of Staff, thus blowing both of their 'covers.' Tom just had to be patient and wait for his sister to respond.

Seems like an awful lot of patience was being demanded of Tom these days and he wasn't sure just how much patience he had in him.

As Tom sat having an afternoon cup of coffee, someone knocked on his front door. Looking through the little 'peep hole' in the door Tom could see two men standing outside waiting for the knock to be answered. Upon a closer look,

Tom determined one of the men to be the police captain he had been phoning, and the other person could be Dr. Chambers; he wasn't sure. Tom opened the door to see Police Captain O'Brien and Dr. Chambers standing there with big smiles on their faces.

"Gentlemen, what brings you to these woods today?" asked Tom.

Captain O'Brien responded that they had both arrived in front of Tom's house at the same time, and, as for himself, he had decided to drop by to give Tom a short driving test and return his driver's license. Dr. Chambers said that he had texted Tom twice about getting a quick update on his vitals before trying to drive, again, but had not gotten any reply. So Dr. Chambers decided to drive by on his way back to the hospital from a meeting in neighboring Fairfield.

Tom invited both men to come in and sit and offered them both some coffee, or something stronger to drink. Dr. Chambers declined Tom's offer but Captain O'Brien said that he would appreciate a cup of coffee.

After Tom got the captain his cup of coffee, Dr. Chambers asked if he could check Tom's vitals and see how his scars were healing. Tom agreed, and sat down on a dining room chair to talk to the police captain while the doctor did his thing. After completing his exam, Dr. Chambers commented on how beautifully Tom's many,

many scars had healed. "Amazing thing, that Super Glue!" Dr. Chambers joked. The police captain looked at the doctor with a puzzled look before looking at Tom. Tom laughed and told the police captain that the hospital was trying to save money so instead of stapling him together, or sewing up all his wounds, they simply 'Super Glued' his body back together.

"Actually, Captain O'Brien the medical field has been using a form of the commercial adhesive Super Glue for many years to stop bleeding, and help to heal cuts and wounds. It started during the Viet Nam War as a fast method for Medics to get bleeding stopped. Also, much easier to carry four times more glue than sutures and such. So, yes, we simply glued Tom Kitchen back together, again. Just like Humpty Dumpty." Dr. Chambers said. He then told Tom that everything looked very good and he could not see any problem with Tom beginning driving again.

With that, Captain O'Brien took Tom's driver's license out of his shirt pocket and handed it to him with a smile. "Guess you might be anxious to get this back, Tom?" the captain said. Tom gladly took the license and put it into his pocket while replying "yes, sir, I sure am. I'm about to run out of food and need to do some grocery shopping. Plus I need to go by and check on my businesses and see if I still have them." The three men laughed together and sat back to discuss various topics for another hour.

Dr. Chambers asked Tom if he recalled anything new about the attack on him, to which Tom said that he had not. Tom had no recall of anything other than the dreams that he had discussed already.

Captain O'Brien told the doctor, and Tom, that the Bridgeport Police Department had found two deceased Latino male bodies floating in the water between the Pleasure Beach Water Taxi and Johnsons Creek. "Both men appear to be members of the Mendoza Mob" the Captain said, "and had the 'signature' tattoos on heir necks. One of the men's fingerprints match prints taken off your belt and wallet when you were brought into the hospital after the attack on you. Any thoughts on this, Tom?"

"No" Tom replied. "How did they die? And, why would one fellow's prints match and no others."

The Captain explained that they were only able to pull five prints, two whole and three partial prints, off of Tom's possessions and all prints were close enough to each other to probably have come from the same person. Probably this dead fellow.

Tom scratched his head and wondered just how much the police would be able to find about his assailants without his being able to recall anything at all. Tom told Captain O'Brien and Dr. Chambers that he had spent a lot of time trying to remember something, any little thing, but had not been able to do so. Dr. Chambers told Tom that often when something so traumatic happens to a person, the brain shuts everything out completely and it could be years before anything about the attack is recalled. If at all.

Dr. Chambers said that he was pleased that Tom was feeling well and his "glued-together" body was holding up well, and that he had to get back to the hospital. With that, both the doctor and the police captain thanked Tom for his hospitality and asked him to contact the police department if anything should be recalled.

Tom assured the captain that he would call, and thanked him for all the help of both him, and the officers of his department.

After both men had departed, Tom decided it was time for him to go to the market and do a decent shopping for groceries.

Singing along, at the top of her lungs, Janice was surprised at how many songs from the 50's and 60's that she knew all the words to. Even though it was before her time, Janice spent a lot of her young years listening to radio stations play the Rock & Roll hits of the day. Her father had bought her a radio of her own and the music was blasted out by station after station for free. Janice and all her girl friends kept up to date with all the big hits. It came in handy when, like today, she had a relatively long drive to make.

Janice pulled into Hartford shortly before noon and was able to find a parking space just a block away from the state office building where she knew the office of vital statistics to be located. So far she was feeling very lucky and she hoped that the good luck would continue to follow her during her research. She grabbed her brief bag, iPhone and its' wall charger and started walking.

When she made her way to the third floor of the building she was surprised to see a large crowd of people waiting in line to search through records. She got into the end of the line to wait her turn. As she stood in line waiting, she studied the people coming and going up and down the hallway. People always amused her with their antics, their being in a full-on race to get somewhere and so something, as well as just being fun to watch.

As Janice stood in line waiting for some measureable forward movement, she heard someone say "CNN? This is the line for the public, not for CNN reporters." She turned to her left to see a feature reporter from the local ABC news team smiling at her.

"I'm serious," he said, "the public stands in line for admission, credentialed media people just go to the back desk, show your ID card, and sign in. Come with me." With that, Janice got out of the long line and followed him through the office doors and to a large desk at the back of the room where sat a rather rotund woman who had not smiled in a very long, long time.

"Show Filamina your CNN ID card and then sign into this book over here. Must be a big story if CNN is investigating things. Can you spill any clues? Anything?" the fellow asked.

Janice finished sign into the registry, turned to look right into his eyes, and said "actually, this is personal research, not CNN. I've discovered some lost relatives, or more correctly, believed-to-be-relatives that I need to research and see if they are related, or not. Nothing for CNN in this task, all my time and money."

He didn't believe Janice, completely, but knew that he would give her room to do whatever it is that she is going to do here. He had his own project to worry about and a rapidly approaching deadline.

"Listen, I'm sorry about coming on so forcefully, I don't care why you're here and it's really none of my business. I don't have time to lend any further assistance. Filamina can answer any questions and give you any help you need, I have a deadline to meet." And with that he went off down a hallway on his left.

Janice found an empty table in the section she needed to be in, so she sat her things down and started searching birth records. Two hours later and she still did not know any more about anyone. Nothing.

So she started on marriages, and all the tons and tons of licenses issued. She read and read until she thought her eyes were going to burn themselves out, so she took a short break and a long walk. A walk that lasted ten minutes and left Janice feeling refreshed and ready to start all over again. When she did, she finished with the marriage licenses which made her sit back and wonder "what now? Where do I go to find something when I don't know what it is that I'm looking for?"

Janice was still sitting back trying to find a new angle when the fellow from ABC News walked by on his way out. He stopped to say goodbye to Janice and ask her if she was okay. "I'm fine just tired of not finding any information on the people I'm searching for. It's almost as if they never existed, and yet I know that they did." Janice told him.

"Well, knowing you, you checked all of the obvious things like births, deaths, marriages. Did you check on adoptions?" He asked as he said his goodbye and headed for the exit.

Adoptions? Thought Janice. Something she had never considered was that one, or more of them, were adopted. She looked at the various signs and did not see any for adoptions, so she got up and walked over to the desk to ask for help. The woman behind the desk told Janice that what ever information was public regarding adoptions, was contained in a different room and gave Janice directions for finding it. "However," the young woman started to say "we close promptly in five minutes, so you'll have to find the room another day." And with that an announcement came over the public address system that the offices would be closing in five minutes.

Janice returned to her work table to gather up her things and call it a day. She would go find an inexpensive motel for the night, and come back in the morning. Cheap motel would be better; as she told the fellow from ABC News "it is her time, it is her dime."

After a poor nights' sleep on an uncomfortable bed, in a very noisy environment, Janice welcomed the stomach-filling, somewhat tasty breakfast she bought at the local Country Waffles restaurant. She thought to herself "there's nothing like strong coffee, and maple syrup to get the system moving." She checked her emails on her iPhone while she enjoyed her second, or maybe third, cup of coffee, then headed out to her car and off to the state building for more exciting research.

This time when she walked into the state office building, she knew exactly what to do. She found the stairs that she could use to get to the third floor. She thought this to be a good way to work off some of the maple syrup that she had consumed this morning. After showing her credentials to Filamina, and signing in on the register, she headed for the hallway that the young woman had told her about yesterday. When she got to the room with the sign above it which read "ADOPTION RECORDS, Public Information Only", she found the door was locked. She knocked lightly at first, following up with several much harder knocks and poundings. No response from inside.

Janice walked back to the front desk and asked Filamina if someone was working inside that room today, and could unlock the door. Filimina slowly looked at Janice over the top of her glasses before saying "no."

Janice simply looked at Filimina for a few seconds before saying "no, what?"

Filimina once again did the slow motion head turn, look over the rim of her glasses at Janice and said "no. Period. No."

Janice did not feel in the mood for whatever game it was that Filimina felt like playing today so she moved about a foot to her left so she would be almost in front of Filimina, bent over the counter slightly and said "who, then, can unlock the door for me. I have research that I need to do in that room."

"Dunno, honey. I got my job. I got my desk. I busy doing my thing."

Now Janice was beginning to feel her body temperature rise and she did not want to let this get into an argument, or a shouting match with someone who had absolutely no interest in Janice or her needs. So Janice stood thinking of how she could re-phrase her words to make them more pleasing to Filimina, and possibly get a little more cooperation from her. As she was standing thinking, she saw a maintenance man pushing a janitor's cart toward the hallway and an idea popped into her head. She quickly left the front desk, and Filimina's dis-interest in her, and followed the maintenance guy down the long hallway.

"Excuse me, sir." Janice called out to him. "Excuse me, but Filimina said you could unlock this door for me since she has so many people to help out front that she cannot leave her desk. Is that correct? Can you unlock it for me? I left my recorder inside yesterday and need to retrieve it." Janice hoped that he would not go ask Filimina for confirmation.

"I'm not supposed to let anyone in unless there's a state worker with them, Ma'am." He responded.

"That's fine, you can go in with me since you're a state worker, can't you?" Janice asked. She was hoping that he would not go in and wait for her to look for something she knew was not there.

"Yeah, I guess I could, but I can't stay very long. I've got to get these supplies downstairs quick. I'll unlock it, you get you 'corder, and we'll leave, fast. Okay?"

All Janice could do was to say "okay", and hope that

she could work something else out in due time.

With the office door opened, and the man standing just inside the doorway, Janice walked in and laid her things on the first table she saw. She pretended to look on chair seats, under tables, around the large filing cabinets which consumed the middle of the room until the maintenance man said that he had to make his delivery downstairs.

"If you want, just propped the door open so anyone can see inside and see what I'm doing, make your delivery downstairs, and come back here. I'm sure I'll have found it by then." Janice hoped that this would sound palatable to him, and it did. He said that he would be back shortly. He said that he would be in the copy room on the first floor and to leave the door wide open. Janice assured him that she would.

After he left, Janice took her mini-recorder out of her brief bag and put it into her jeans pocket before starting to go through records of adoptions. She hurried trying to cover more names, faster than she would normally try to in case the man came back early.

Thinking she heard him coming down the hallway, she stopped and looked outside the office door, only to see two people go into a restroom further down the hall. It was then she noticed a map of the state buildings above the desk phone in the room and an idea came to her. She looked at a list of names and phone extension numbers posted next to the map, took down a name, crossed her fingers, and made a phone call to the copy room.

Claiming to be "Sharon Lewis" she told the person who answered the phone in the copy room, that she had just sent the maintenance guy down with their needed supplies, and it was now very important that he go to "room 503 in the assembly building. There are some envelopes there that are urgently needed over in the Capital in room 701." She tried to sound as professional, and dis-interested as she could. The fellow on the other end of the phone asked if he could repeat it back to her to be certain that he had it right. "Thank God", she thought to herself. "Yes, that's correct. From room 503 over to room 701. Thank you". Hoping she had bought a little more time she hung up the phone, closed the door and went back to work searching.

Janice hardly noticed it but almost two hours later, she looked up to see bright rays of sun come booming into the room. She looked at her watch and guessed that her little ploy had worked. But, she thought, she is probably running out of time quickly.

It was about then that she came across copies of records that startled her. Janice didn't notice the name 'Poston' when scanning the records, but as she scanned further she did notice the last name 'Eldon.' She read carefully, and re-read just as carefully to find that a three year old, Jerry Poston, and a one year old, Jeffrey Poston were both adopted by Dr. Milton Eldon, PHD, and an anonymous female. Janice remembered meeting Dr. Helen Eldon and her husband Dr. Milton Eldon at a hospital dedication in Bridgeport. Janice was certain that these must all be the same people! There couldn't be other people with the same exact names and city.

Janice took photos of the records with her iPhone and put them back into the file to continue looking. While she searched through more records, the question kept coming to her mind about the term "anonymous female." Why would Milton Eldon NOT list his wife by name? This puzzled Janice a lot but, it was not something she had to unravel right now.

Right now she had to hurry with her investigation because she could hear voices talking off down the long hallway land knew that she would have company soon. She read reports rapidly, made copious verbal notes in her mini-recorder, took a few more photos with her iPhone before picking up her things and putting them in her brief bag.

Minutes later the maintenance man walked into the room with a state patrolman at his side. The patrolman asked what Janice was doing, to which she replied that she was waiting for the other fellow to return so she could leave after finding her recorder that she had left in the room yesterday. The patrolman asked for Janice's recorder and began to check her recordings on it. Janice had anticipated this and had left several minutes recorded about some search for her relatives that did not materialize in the adoption records.

Satisfied, the patrolman gave Janice her recorder back and asked if she was ready to leave so he could escort her out. 'Escort her out?' she thought. She is a credentialed news reporter, Peabody Award and Emmy winner, an adult in a public building, "why do you have to escort me anywhere?" she asked. She felt that she was within her rights asking, but the patrolman simply stood looking at Janice as if she spoke a foreign language.

"You're in a closed records room without permission, so I need to assist you in finding the exit to the street." The state patrolman answered.

"Now just a minute!" Janice responded. "I was escorted to this room, the door unlocked by this man to look for my property that I left here yesterday, and I have been waiting here all this time for him to return. I didn't want to leave here with the door being unlocked because I told him I would wait here for him to return. He was only going to be gone a couple minutes, he told me."

The patrolman asked the other fellow if all this is true or not, to which the maintenance man said it is. He also added that "someone phoned the copy room and had them send me on a 'wild goose' chase which delayed me getting right back up here."

The state trooper thought for a minute before apologizing to Janice for thinking that she might be an intruder, and that she was free to leave.

Janice gathered up all her things, wished both men a 'good day', and headed for the outdoors and her parked car. She has a lot of notes and information to go through, and to piece together to see if there is any connection from one item to another, and she would love to sit down and do it right now while things are fresh in her mind, but she is going somewhere quiet where she can concentrate. With that desire in mind, Janice decided to head for a public library and see if she can accomplish things there.

Her dime, her time.

CHAPTER 18

Tom did not hate New York City, he only hated the massive crowds that one had to deal with when trying to get out of Grand Central Station and find a taxi to go somewhere. Constant pushing, shoving, getting bumped into, just made Tom furious and he had to talk to himself to stay calm. The one thing about all this is, that if a person is trying to hide out, do it in downtown Manhattan. There, because of these same huge crowds.

Tom caught a cab and gave the driver the address of 599 Broadway in lower Manhattan; the address of the American Eagle Outfitters store where he is to meet his sister Helen. Seems things are moving much more rapidly for both of them than they thought that they would, so meeting day and time had to be moved forward.

Tom paid the driver, exited the taxi and walked into the store. A store selling clothes to people much, much younger than he, and with totally different taste in styles. He looked around and was aware of all the looks that he was getting. Tom thought to himself "you don't feel old until someone much younger just stares at you like you have a case of leprosy, and suddenly you feel as though you're one-hundred and ten.

Tom walked over to the 'boys' section and began to look through shirts, not surprised that he didn't find anything to his liking. He continued to look around and finally did find some tee shirts that were something that he would wear, and possibly buy.

He continued looking at more clothes, this time in the men's section and was examining a plaid shirt when a voice behind him softly said "you won't find trout fishing gear in this type of store, mister."

Tom turned around to see the eyes and smile of his sister Helen, but the body, clothes, hair and makeup of someone he could not identify. "Helen?" he asked. "I can't believe that it's you."

His sister put her finger to her lips and gave a "shhhhh" motion and told him her name is Rosie. "Rosie Johnson, sir, and I work here, so I can answer any questions you might have about our clothes."

Tom looked around and saw both other employees looking their way, as well as customers peering in their general direction. He showed her the shirt that he was holding and asked her if they might have it in size XL, because the shirt he held was only a medium.

Rosie Johnson said she would check for him and left to go off the sales floor toward the back of the store. Tom continued to look through other clothes and found another shirt that he might consider buying that was in his XL size. A few minutes later Rosie returned with a couple shirts and showed them to Tom. He actually liked one of them and asked if he could buy the two shirts he held. But first, he wanted to try each one on to see if the company's sizing matched his body sizing.

Rosie pointed him toward the fitting rooms and said that she would check on him in a few minutes. Tom was happy that both shirts fit him well and decided to buy both. A rare shopping trip for him, as he never took the time to shop for anything other than necessities like food, and such.

Tom exited the fitting room and found Rosie standing just outside waiting. He told her he wanted to buy both shirts and handed them to her. She, in turn, handed Tom a business card with her name on it and said she would 'ring them up' for Tom if he was done shopping. Tom told her he was done and they both headed for the cash register.

When Tom finished paying for his shirts, he walked out of the store, made a left turn and walked about two hundred feet down the street before stopping. He took the business card out of his pocket and read the back: '1 hour dinner break in 15 minutes. Meet me 3 blocks east at Coin-O-Matic Café.' Tom looked at his watch and determined that he had ten minutes left. Tom started walking east until he found the café and waited for Rosie.

It was only a few minutes later that Rosie came around the corner of the building and told Tom to follow her. She continued walking for another block to a small, family owned and operated pizza-by-the-slice café where they could sit in a corner and have a slice of pizza and a glass of Chianti, and talk.

After the young man delivered their pizza and wine to them and left, Tom told Helen, er, Rosie, that he had a photo showing that Gilbert was dead down in Nicaragua. He didn't know when it happened, but he is certain he knows how and who did it. He asked Rosie why the disguise and hiding in a clothing store.

Rosie sat still and quiet for a few minutes looking downward at her slice of pizza. Finally she looked up at Tom with watering-up eyes and said "I don't know if you read about the bombing that occurred on the train about five weeks ago, or not, but both Milton, and my son Jeff were on that train. They were returning to their teaching jobs at NYU when the bomb went off. Tom, they never were able to find enough of either one to fill a tea cup. They were among the nineteen people killed, and then shortly after that I received a note at the hospital saying that I was next. Now I do not know if it was someone's sick idea of a joke, or not, but I panicked and fled Bridgeport. I had to get somewhere and hide. I left a couple notes for you but I heard that you were in the hospital near death, so I thought maybe they had already gotten to you. I ran. I ran and hid in the biggest place I could get to; New York City, got a job at the clothes store and am staying low. Did they get to you? Is that why you were in the hospital?"

First, Tom told her how sorry he was to learn about Milton's and Jeff's deaths, and then he told her about his reoccurrence of Malaria forcing him into a short stay in the hospital. Tom also told her about someone injecting him with something that knocked him out and while he was hallucinating, or dreaming about things, they attacked him with knives and almost killed him. He explained that the two were separate stays in the hospital and he was sure that they were not related. Tom asked about her other son, Jerry and his wife and family.

"I don't know," she answered, "I can't get in touch with him for fear that they might be watching him, also. If they are, they would go after him, Shirley and their two children. I can't have that happen. And, as if this was not enough, there is a news reporter from CNN who is asking more, and more, question about Keeper House murders, and the Keeper family. Have you met this Janice Wilkins yet?"

Tom explained that he had only had brief, very short talks with her and had not been 'caught' by her for a full interview, yet.

"Frankly, Tom, I don't know how much longer I can go on with this charade. I hate this look, but I'm too old for them to hire 'a natural', so I have to keep this up to keep some money coming in. Fortunately, they needed people who would show up each day for work so badly that, once I changed my appearance, they hired me right away. Also I'm staying at Jeff's apartment which he had prepaid his rent some six month out. Otherwise, I'd be up that well known creek. Any ideas?"

Tom shook his head 'no.' He knew something had to be done, what did not know is what it was going to be. "I can get money for you to help, but I think for the time being that you will have to keep up with your disguise and wait things out. As for me, I don't know what I will be able to do. If they are getting close to us, I may have to go deeply underground, myself."

They continued eating their pizza and finished off their wine. Tom debated whether, or not, to order more wine, or pizza, but Rosie said that she could not go back to work smelling like a winery. She might get fired. Tom decided that he would get another slice and glass of wine anyway since he was not returning to work.

Tom asked his sister if she had gotten the 'jewelry' that he had fashioned for her which contained the much-needed, oddly-shaped, key. She confirmed that she did receive it and is wearing it under her top right now. She said she is afraid to leave it anywhere for fear that it will disappear. Tom added that he had to get the rest of the 'documents' to her for safe keeping, but he did not know how he would accomplish that. He smiled at Rosie and told her that she would be "the keeper of it all. The keys, the documents, the proof of what happened and who is guilty.

Keeper of it all."

Rosie looked at her watch and realized that she had to start walking back to work now, or be late. She told Tom that she found her list of codes that they developed as kids, and would send him messages now and then to stay in touch.

Tom asked her how he should get money to her safely. He wondered if she set up a new bank account somewhere, or if some other method should be used.

"For right now, until I decide what I'm going to do, probably best to use Western Union and wire it to me here in the City. Wait! I don't have any 'state-issued' photo identification to be able to pick it up from Western Union when it's received. Can you disguise it some way and ship it UPS to Jeff's address where I'm staying?"

Tom said he would handle it, and code it to her as to how it's coming. With that, Tom and Rosie got up and gave each other a big, long-lasting, hug and kiss on the cheek before Rosie left to head back to her place of work.

Tom decided to stay and relax for a few minutes while finishing his wine and pizza. This relaxation time might be good for Tom, and enable him to come up with a good solution for Helen, or Rosie's, situation.

Janice Wilkins leaned back in the straight-back library chair she was using and exhaled slowly. Unable to believe the picture that she was assembling with all the notes, photos and other bits of information being put together, she simply leaned back and sighed quietly. It was becoming clearer to her what had happened in the old Victorian house known as Keeper House, and who was involved with the event. Even with facts staring right at her, she still had to double and triple check everything to make herself believe.

Some facts that tied things together fit into the puzzle strictly by accident, in that, they were derived from police reports, back-page newspaper stories, and other minor sources. Janice had been careful in her research, but obviously she had also been lucky while doing it. She was intrigued by a very small, about five line story on the very back page of the local paper dealing with incest in Westport. While it did not mention any names, there was another story in the Bridgeport paper about a wealthy Westport man being arrested, and released from custody, for child pornography and illegal activities with minors. Again, no names were mentioned in this article either.

While Janice was able to see a clear picture being formed from her investigations, she was still anxious to return to Bridgeport or Westport, and interview people that she thought were, or could be, involved with this story. She would pick up everything and leave now, except the dinner hour was quickly approaching and she felt better getting a room for tonight and leaving tomorrow. Right now she needed to make copies of her notes, photos, recordings, and all her other data; she didn't want to lose any of it, nor have it taken from her. She thought she would head off for the closest Kinko's store and put her mind at ease. Next, she would check in at the motel where she had stayed before, and then get some dinner.

Dr. Walker really enjoyed his thriving medical practice and was thankful every morning that he and his wife had made the decision to make the move to New Haven and that he went into partnership with the retiring Dr. Greybar. He enjoyed their new lifestyle so much that he didn't even give any thought to interviewing for a position at the Montgomery & Eloise Walker Children's Medical Center when the hospital called and asked him to. He didn't tell his wife about the invitation, yet, as he knew that she had finally settled in and found places for everything that they had moved from Rhode Island. He definitely would tell her about the invite but that would come later.

He did, however, phone Dr. Chambers at the hospital to get some input from a doctor that he had met before, and who is practicing medicine at the hospital. He enjoyed his brief conversation with Dr. Chambers, but the doctor did not say anything which enticed Dr. Walker into considering taking the interview. He did find out, though, that the Chief of Staff of the Children's Hospital, Dr. Helen Eldon, has been missing after taking a leave-of-absence from her position there. No one knows her where abouts and it is presumed that she has met with an untimely death. To date, though, nothing has been confirmed.

Dr. Walker has grown the business a great deal since joining Dr. Greybar, and has gotten the contract with the local school district to give all prospective athletes, for all high school sports, their required physicals. He explained his procedures and recommendations to the school board and they liked how complete and detailed his exams would be for the cost-per-student. That was the good news; the other side of this coin is that now Dr. Walker must hire an additional, or hopefully two, more nurses to handle the patient load. Time to start interviewing, and to promote his number one employee, Amanda, to a higher, more involved and sharing the rewards, position of General Manager. He liked that idea and made a note on his calendar to meet with Amanda and get her thoughts on it.

He was also looking at the probability that Dr. Greybar would have his full, and final payment before the end of year four instead of at the end of year five as agreed.

It was this thought that Dr. Walker was enjoying when his receptionist buzzed him on the phone saying his wife was calling. He took the call and listened to her very intently as she described something to him.

"Where did they take him?" he asked his wife. "I'm just about to see Mrs. Fitzpatrick for her annual exam. When I finish, I'll adjust the rest of the day and leave. How is my Mother doing? Good. Did they check her BP and vitals when they arrived? Okay, I'll see you there." With that call ending, Dr. Walker went off to exam room 4, and Mrs. Fitzpatrick.

Later that morning Dr. Walker had the balance of the day rearranged so that Amanda could handle most of the remaining patients, leaving a few that would have to be rescheduled.

Gerald Walker guided his car onto the Interstate and pointed it south for Bridgeport and the medical center there. He knew the thirty minute drive would seem like a lot longer, but when he gets a call that his elderly father and mother have fallen down a flight of stairs in their home and have been taken to the hospital in serious condition, Gerald will shorten that travel time.

Carl and Carla Walker were already at the hospital when Gerri Walker arrived with her children. She found the children's care ward and made arrangements for the four children to stay there under the supervision of the floor nurse as she went looking for information about her in-laws. She knew that Gerald was on his way, but Gerri Walker had developed such a deep love for her in-laws that she was not going to wait for her husband or anyone else. She got the room numbers for both Mr. Walker, and his wife, and headed for that floor. Dr. Chambers was coming out of Mrs. Walker's room when Gerri Walker came down the hallway approaching the room.

"I'm sorry, Mrs. Walker, but you can't go in there right now." Dr. Chambers told her. "I've just given her a sedative to help her get some sleep, and I've put her on a 'drip' for her pain. Give her two to three hours rest and then we'll see about visitors. Please tell the rest of your family the same thing as I will be having this wing of the floor sealed off and secured."

Gerri Walker understood, although she did not like not be able to see her mother in law, that Mrs. Walker's health was of the utmost importance right now. She asked how her father in law, Mr. Walker was doing before turning to leave the area. Dr. Chambers walked along side Gerri telling her that he is very concerned about Mr. Walker because he suffered the greater damage from the fall. "Apparently, Mr. Walker started to fall," Dr. Chambers said, "and his wife, who was walking with him, grabbed onto him and they tumbled down several stairs before Mrs. Walker grabbed onto the railing. At that moment, Mr. Walker just continued to tumble freely on down the stairs ending up on the next level unconscious. We are estimating that it could have been as long as fifteen to thirty minutes before they were discovered by a man who stopped by to work on Mrs. Hunter's grandfather clock. Right now, I'm waiting on Mr. Walker to become more stable so we can run more tests to learn the full extent of his internal injuries. He is in a room on this floor, but I've already isolated him, so he cannot have any visitors yet, either."

Again, Gerri was not happy, but understood that it was not her desires that had to be met, but the well-being of her in-laws. "Thank you, Dr. Chambers, I will go meet the other family members and update them on what you have told me. My husband will be here any minute, and I'm sure he will want to talk directly to you when he arrives. Will that be okay?"

"That is fine with me, except that I have to be in surgery in twenty minutes so he may have to scrub up." Dr. Chambers smiled slightly and told Gerri that he would see her shortly when he has more news.

Gerri turned the corner and started walking down the long hallway which would lead her to the visitor's waiting room.

Tom Kitchen was heading back to his Ace Hardware store after explaining to the police, the EMT's, a doctor, and a reporter from the local newspaper, that he was stopping by Keeper House on a routine service call arranged by Mrs. Hunter months ago, to work on her grandfather clock. He tried to make them understand that they knew he would be by at a preset time, and they expected him. On previous calls, when they were not at home, or busy on their boat, they would simply leave the front door unlocked and he would go into the entryway and perform his service work on the clock. So this time was no different; after no answer from his many knocks on the front door, or from his many rings of the doorbell, he opened the front door, took his toolbox and entered the entryway to do his work. It was while he was starting to tune the clock's movement that he heard some moaning from within and eventually saw Mr. and Mrs. Walker laying on different levels of the long staircase. He checked them both to see if they were breathing, or not , and called 9-1-1.

After Stephanie Hunter confirmed with the police everything that Tom Kitchen had said, Tom left for his hardware store, and Stephanie, and her husband Derek, left for the hospital in Bridgeport.

What Tom did not tell anyone about, not even Stephanie Hunter, was the horrendous smell of rotting meat that permeated the entire front of Keeper House when he arrived. Tom also did not tell her that a big earthquake was occurring as he enter the house and could have been the cause of the Walkers falling down the stairs. He had a vague recollection of that happening when he was a child visiting there, but would not spend much time thinking about those days. At least, not right now.

Tom decided, when he got to the hardware store, that he would send Rosie some things as a 'trial' to see if his method was going to work. He took copies of some of the documents, put them into a box along with some money, and prepared them for shipment via UPS. He was well aware of some of the problems that have occurred with shipments being stolen after delivery, but he was going to test this anyway. He doubled check the address where Rosie is staying before printing out a label for the box.

Tom thought about staying at the hardware store and getting some more work done, but he saw the reporter from CNN outside his back room asking for the manager. Tom decided it was time to head out the back door before she found him.

Gerri Walker found the visitor's waiting room full of family members just as she saw her husband Gerald walking up the hallway toward her. She waved at Gerald and walked into the open arms of Stephanie and Derek. Everyone was up out of their chairs waiting for Gerri's update of what she knew. Everyone had been stopped by the nurses, and the locked, section doors, from going into the ward areas after being told that there was already one family member talking to Dr. Chambers.

Gerri started telling everyone what the doctor had told her about both parents, stopped momentarily to give her husband a hug and kiss when he walked into the room, and then resumed with her talk. Gerald Walker listened, asked a question or two, then asked where Dr. Chambers was at. Gerri told her husband that he would have to 'scrub up' in order to talk with Dr. Chambers to which he said that the operating room was not the place to have that type of talk. He would wait until after the operation was completed.

One-by-one the Walkers arrived, met with other family members in the waiting room and waited to get updates on their parent's condition. It was about an hour and a half later, that Gerald Walker heard his name being called over the hospital paging system and left to find a phone.

It took about fifteen minutes before Gerald Walker returned to the waiting room to inform the family members of their parents' condition. "It is not looking good for either one of our parents," he started saying. "Both Mom and Dad suffered severe damages in their falls, both are clinging to life right now, and our father is going to have to have another operation to alleviate internal bleeding and relieve cranial swelling that he is experiencing. It will be several hours before anything new is known, so, not all of us can stay and wait because of our children. I think those of us who can stay, should. The rest should take care of others who need them, and we all should spend some time praying. Prayers will definitely be needed today." With that, half of the family decided to go take care of business, or children, or other matters and wait for further updates to be passed along to them. Carl, Carla and Dr. Gerald decided that they would stay and wait for information to come from the team of doctors, and then they would update other family members.

Helen, or Rosie Johnson, sent Tom a coded message indicating she had received his package. Tom knew she was frightened beyond words, especially after what had happened to her husband and youngest son, but Tom also knew that they had to keep struggling and stay alive until the truth was known to the whole world. Tom would now make arrangements to have copies of all the 'important' documents, and other evidence, shipped to Rosie for safe keeping. The siblings had also made arrangement a few years ago to have copies of evidence items stored in a secure, neutral, location whose only whereabouts is contained in letters locked inside the safes in Tom's offices in the Ace Hardware, and his "About Time" clock shop.

Tom was focused on getting Helen taken care of, and safe, but he had not yet calmed down from the horrendous murder of his brother Gerald in Nicaragua. He knew that he would get even with Ernesto Siguenya, and as many Mendoza Mob members as he could, in some way, in time.

He wasn't sure how he would do it, but he knew that the time was coming. That thought stuck with him for a few minutes and gave him cause to wonder. "Time was coming", he thought.

Maybe there is a way he can get it done.

CHAPTER 19

This is the type of day that anyone, and everyone, is glad to be alive, and have the day envelope them from head to toe. The weatherman forecasted temperatures in the low-to-mid seventies, and it is seventy two. Winds of six to ten miles per hour produced nothing more than a warm, and gentle breeze, and the air was clear and contained just a hint of the aromas of blooming flowers. Nearly perfect in every respect for anyone having to be outdoors, but for anyone, or a small group of family members, having to be inside a hospital waiting room, it was certainly a gloomy and dank day everywhere.

The doctors at St. Vincent's Medical Center were trying, as much as they could, to minimize the flow of bad news to family members. But when people want updates, and the news is nothing but bad, as one doctor put it "the river of news only flows one direction."

The news that bothered Dr. Gerald Walker the most is that both his mother and father had suffered massive hematomas, and Mr. Walker has other complications with which the doctors have to deal. He has suffered repeated internal bleeding and shows many ecchymoses, or large diameter blood bruises on his back, arms and chest areas. If he fought a battle with all the steps in that flight from the second floor to the third, the stairs won, and Mr. Walker lost.

Mr. Walker was about to undergo his third operation in search of the bleeding problem, and the doctors were not as optimistic as Gerald Walker would like them to be. Dr. Gerald knew, from close conferences with the team of doctors attending to Mr. Walker, that the news was not getting better. He began to wonder if he should begin preparing his family members for the inevitable news that may be forthcoming. He fought with himself over this question and decided that he would not do it, yet. He knew that in the world of medicine that there is always hope.

While much focus was being paid to the family patriarch, Mr. Walker, Mrs. Walker was not fairing any better. Her doctor was fearing that her age, and frail skeletal condition would not favor her for a quick recovery. She had suffered many broken bones, and a cracked rib had punctured a lung causing respiratory problems for her. Her doctor told the family that it was "touch and go" with Mrs. Walker for now, and with every hour that passed she was getting better.

Stephanie and Derek told the family members that everyone should get some rest and come to their house for dinner; nothing formal, just an "informal, kick off our shoes and relax" kind of dinner. "The kids can watch movies, or play games if they want, and the adults can talk and relax while we await more news from the doctors."

Everyone agreed and the women all got together to

determine what each family could bring to help with dinner. A time was agreed upon, and a menu put together from each family's specialty. Stephanie hoped that everyone would get together, relax, and lose some of their stress they felt from their parents' mishap.

Dr. Gerald Walker talked to Dr. Chambers before the family left the hospital waiting room giving him cell phone numbers, as well as Stephanie's home phone numbers. Dr. Chambers felt that what the family was doing would definitely help all of them, and he would contact them with any update.

The dinner was exactly as Stephanie described it would be: informal. Relaxing, with more food than could possibly be consumed, and an endless supply of wine and other spirits. The children played computer games and laughed out loud, and the adults talked about a 'hundred and one' topics as they drank their drinks.

Derek Hunter took advantage of being home to get some paperwork done so he could fax it back to his office in the morning. Seems Sorrabon Publishing had signed an agreement with a new fiction, mystery writer from northern California. Derek liked his novels, and especially the fact that they were all set in the Connecticut and New England region. He always enjoyed reading about something that could have happened in his own backyard, so to speak. Derek finished his tasks and went out to the family room to join the other adults, and his glass of wine.

The conversations were going strong; talk about politics, talking about children, talking about vacation plans, and the occasional joke telling which brought some moments of laughter. It was a fun, warm and loving atmosphere until the phone started ringing.

At the precise moment of the first ring of the phone, a complete, and bone chilling, quiet came over the room. Even the children stopped their fun and just sat and looked out into the foyer as if they expected to see a horrible monster appear. The second ring of the phone was not any louder than the first had been, although it seemed to rattle the walls and make everything vibrate and rattle.

Finally, Derek got up from his chair and answered the phone as the third ring started. He did not say anything, he simply listened. No one could tell by the lack of expression on Derek's face if it was good news, or bad news on the phone. Derek didn't say much at all until he said "okay, doctor. Thank you for calling. I will tell the rest of the family." As he hung up the phone, he simply stared at the front door for several seconds before turning and heading into the dining room where everyone else was gathered.

By now, most of the color had drained from Derek's face and his voice was strained and shaking when he looked at Stephanie and the gathered family members and said, "that was Dr. Chambers calling. Mr. Walker died quietly about an hour ago from complications from the accident. He suffered much more internal damage than anticipated, and at his age, was not able to recover from all of it. More over, just seventeen minutes after Mr. Walker died, Mrs. Walker also stopped breathing and passed into a very peaceful death. So, tonight we have lost both of our beloved parents." Although Derek was not born a Walker, he always felt as though they were his parents because of the way they loved and treated him throughout his courtship years, and married years, to Stephanie.

The news was devastating to everyone and it also effected the children. Hearing Derek tell the adults the news, started the older children crying. That, of course, got the younger children crying. Soon everyone in the entire house was crying, some without knowing exactly why they were doing so. Just that others were, so they would, too.

It took eight-to-ten minutes before all the sobbing and sniffling ended and the children began asking why everyone was so unhappy. Derek looked to Gerald and Gerri as if to ask them if he should answer the child's question, or not. Gerri decided that she would take all the children into another room and explain what had happened to their grandparents. Answer their questions, and give them time to absorb the words and their meaning. This might take some time, so Gerri told the others to continue discussions without her.

Derek decided that this was a good time for everyone to have a refill of their favorite beverage; some might even opt for something stronger.

Tom had sent the last of the 'documents' to Rosie for safe keeping and told her that she was now "the keeper of it all." Everything that all the Keeper children had held onto for so many years, was now in her hands. He also told her in a coded message that back up copies existed, and where they were hidden.

While Tom Kitchen had always been most fond of the hardware store, he loved 'fooling around' with clocks and learning about some of the great timepieces and how they functioned. He also liked and appreciated electronics as a youngster so he was glad when he was given the opportunity to buy the local electronics supply store. Although it never produced income like the clock shop or the hardware store did, he still enjoyed access to things electric when he needed them. And he felt like he really needed some of them now. Right now!

As Tom finished his last little 'project', he didn't know whether to feel good, or not.

Tom grabbed his suitcase and loaded it, along with all the boxes he had, into his Jeep. He decided it was time to leave for New Haven and begin phase 1. After New Haven, he will head for Hartford and phase 2. At one point Tom had considered maybe going further east to Boston, but decided that he would feel more confident doing this project from Hartford, rather than Boston. He found a small inexpensive room at a local motel, and started researching local hiring halls. Tom would end up calling a couple in the morning to hire some young college kid, or teenage boy, to deliver his boxes.

Tom had already done a lot of research into how much each carton would cost to ship from various locations, as well as a lot of other information he will be needing.

Tom got a good night's sleep and was ready when morning came; coffee and a couple donuts that he brought with him and he would be off. He had already found a delivery company that would be delivering his packages, both to addressees, and to the local UPS store.

Tom's plan was simple: he had assembled several clocks, and cell phones, into bombs and was having them sent to various businesses, and people, who belonged to the Mendoza Mob. He had gotten names, addresses and other pertinent information from various sources and had put this plan together after seeing his sister Helen. He knew that Helen and he could not live their lives in constant fear of being found by the mob, plus he was given information that linked the Mendoza Mob to his brother's death in Nicaragua. And, yes, Tom has a 'special' package to be delivered to Ernesto Siguenya that Tom knew he would get a real bang out of. Sixteen. Sixteen special packages to be delivered to Tom's list of 'special' people. Now Tom had to get started with phase one of his plan.

The young delivery fellow showed up exactly on time to pick up the first five cartons from Tom, and deliver them to the local FedEx store for shipping out. Tom went over the instructions very carefully and gave him the cash to make everything happen. Tom also included a healthy tip for the fellow, along with the cell phone number of Tom's 'burner' phone he purchased for the shipping, and delivery, confirmations to come back to. Phase one of the plan had begun for Tom; time to check out of his room and drive to Hartford. A quick forty five minute drive that would give Tom some time for thinking about his future, and the future he wanted for Helen.

Tom stopped for a quick breakfast before getting on Interstate 91 and the drive north to Hartford.

Again, Tom repeated all the steps he had taken in New Haven with a small, local delivery company. The young fellow seemed a little confused by the five small cartons and what he had to do, so Tom gave him a copy of the instructions which he had printed out before leaving home. When the fellow read the printed instructions he became immediately clear on his task. Again Tom gave him cash and a healthy tip for his services along with the cell phone number for confirmations. After the young man left Tom's motel room, Tom thought for a couple minutes about some way to double-check this guy to be certain things were handled correctly. Finally, Tom decided that he would wait until tomorrow and see if he got the necessary confirmations before doing anything else. Now for Tom it was time to head off to New London and the third, and final phase of his plan.

It is an hour's drive from Hartford to New London which takes one through some very pretty Connecticut countryside on state route 2. It also gave Tom time to think about what he was doing and how this would effect the balance of criminal activity in New England. No time for guilt feelings, he was working hard to help law enforcement departments lessen the number of criminals; "working people" someone once said, "but on the wrong side of the laws."

Arriving in New London, Tom had already checked into his motel room, and arranged for the pickup time for the delivery company to stop by.

Tom went through the same talk about the directions that he had done twice before, but this time the older man standing there had his own set of questions. Why? Who are these people? Several more that, en total, were none of his damn business Tom thought. Rather than get into a debate with this fellow, Tom carefully avoided answering any of his questions and simply gave him the necessary instructions. Finally, the man picked up the five boxes and left Tom's motel room. "Whew", Tom thought to himself, phase three is completed and now he needed to catch I-95 south, and start the one hour and twenty minute drive home; home to anxiously await the confirmations coming in from the sixteen deliveries.

First, though, Tom would get something to eat for dinner, as he had skipped lunch in Hartford, and was now starving. Off to find a good, casual, diner.

Rosie Johnson, a.k.a. Helen Eldon, was not enjoying her job in retail, but knew she needed it to keep her life's disguise in place. She disliked the people that she had to be nice to, as much, or more, than she disliked all the managers, and assistant managers above her in the 'pecking order.' When she was studying medicine, she had a part time job in retail and totally disliked it for many of the same reasons. She told herself that it was not her, it was simply that people, who come into stores to shop, always leave their manners, and their respect for other people, somewhere else. They never bring any evidence of either into the retail outlet.

Rosie was busy re-stocking shelves with winter, wool shirts that were going to be on sale come the next weekend. She knew that the store would be super busy then and was thankful that she had Saturday off. She didn't really need the hours since Tom had sent her money, so she was very willing to give 'Sale Saturday' to a younger, hungrier college student. Rosie would use that day to organize the documents that Tom had sent her, with her money, and get them into a safe hiding place.

Rosie wonder what sort of plan her brother Tom was working on, and worried about his safety. Tom always had a short fuse and she hoped that he would not go off 'half cocked' and get hurt by someone. Her problem was: she did not know exactly who the 'someone' was, or would be. Is it someone she knows? Is it someone that Tom knows, and she doesn't? Is it a complete stranger, or strangers? Working retail, and dealing with the public, she could be approached at any time and killed. Her saving factor was that she was not recognizable as Dr. Helen Eldon; physically, or otherwise.

Rosie Johnson's life now had no resemblance to any part of her previous life as Helen Eldon. Rosie went to work at various times, and would go home when she was told that she was done for the day. She stayed inside her Westside apartment, fixed her own meals, and watched cable TV, when the cable worked. She had no pets, did not even attempt to make friends with any neighbors, and just stayed to herself.

Her bosses saw much more ability, and intelligence, in Rosie than they expected she had when they hired her. So they cut her some slack with their rules, and such, so that she stayed happy, and stayed with them. She is the type of employee that no employer wants to lose.

Staying very much to herself, Rosie was very surprised when asked out on a date by an older regional manager. Not wanting to anger him, she made up a story, some of which is true, about her just losing her husband and son in an airplane crash and she doesn't feel as though she is ready to date yet. Rosie sold it with such sincerity that the manager said he understood completely, and if she ever just wanted to have dinner with someone one evening, he would be available.

Rosie received nine more shipments from her brother Tom, and each one contained more money than the previous shipment had. She had received enough money from her brother to last her several years, and she hoped that he was not draining his savings to help her. Another problem was looming, also, and that was a safe place in which to put all the cash. Apartment break-ins in the Westside of Manhattan were as frequent as weather changes; maybe, more often. Rosie decided that she would venture out to visit a short list of banks to inquire about opening her necessary accounts.

There were many days when Rosie longed to be Helen again; to be interviewing brilliant young doctors, reviewing research papers, interacting with people she considered much more intelligent than the retail shoppers she was dealing with. These were very difficult days for Rosie to handle, and would send her off into a world of dreaming about how life used to be, and how she wanted it to be, again.

When Rosie started opening her savings accounts, she decided that, in order to prevent 'red flags' from being raised by an unusually large amount of money being deposited, she would open accounts in several local financial institutions. She wanted to keep the largest amount in a close, convenient bank branch for ease of accessing money when she needed to. Rosie decided that CitiBank had the greatest number of ATMs in her area, and ATMs would allow her quick and easy deposits and withdrawals for cash as she needed it.

Fortunately for Rosie, brother Tom had used his contacts to obtain false identification documents for her before he started sending her money and documents. She was able to prove to anyone asking that she was, in fact, Rosie Johnson, born in Gary, Indiana. She was so thankful that she has a brother as smart as Tom who thinks of these types of things before they are needed.

With many savings accounts opened, three sets of documents safely stored in safety deposit boxes, and another six months renewal on her son's apartment done, Rosie settled into her daily existence; her retail existence.

She often thought about quitting her job and living off the money that Tom was furnishing, but she quickly abandoned those thoughts. Beside, management seemed, to her, to like her hard working attitude and kept giving her more, and more, responsibility.

One morning, after Rosie had clocked into work, her store manager called her into his office. Naturally, she thought all the worst possible thoughts that any employee could think, and guessed that it must be that mean, old woman that cussed Rosie out two days ago for not having a blouse in the color that she wanted it in, even though it was never made in that color.

She cautiously opened his office door and asked if he wanted to see her now, or later. He asked her to come in and have a seat. She knew she was history, now.

"Rosie, how are you doing this morning?" he asked. Yep! History! She told herself that "look out unemployment line, her comes Rosie!"

She answered that she was doing well, and thanked him for asking.

He continued, "Good. One of the shortcomings of management, quite often, is not having, or not taking, the time to simply sit and talk with their employees. Especially their most valuable employees. We all need to understand what each other's needs are in life, besides just the regular paychecks. This is always a problem for management, and, I, for one, am sorry about it. You well know how hectic and busy it can get in this place, thus preventing us from just sitting down and talking with each other. I wanted to take a few minutes to tell you how much I like you, how much I value you, both as a person and as an employee, and how much I enjoy the brief talks we have had." Rosie adjusted her position on the straight back chair, and waited for the anvil to land on her head. She knew she is history, now, with a capital "H"!

Her manager took a file folder off the top of his desk and opened it before continuing with "this company is always looking to expand; to spotlight good employees, and to promote from within. That being said, the Board of Directors have asked me to ask you if you would accept a promotion. They would like you to transfer to our store at Union Square West as the assistant store manager. You would continue in that capacity for six to eleven months and then, if you want to be, they would promote you to store manager."

Yep! Rosie knew she was history. She thought briefly about where she should look for another job, or why bother with retail, anyway? Wait! What did he just say? Assistant store manager? Union Square West store? Rosie wasn't sure that she was hearing things correctly.

"Sir, I'm sorry. Did you say assistant store manager at

the Union Square store? I can't believe I heard that." Rosie replied.

Her manager chuckled lightly, and repeated everything he had been saying. He also added the other benefits that Rosie would be receiving being both a full time employee, and a management-level employee. He also covered all the fringe benefits that come with management level status and asked her if she wanted to take some time to think it over.

"Thank you, sir," Rosie answered, "but I don't need any time. I will accept the offer and transfer. I would love to advance upward within this company and learn more about the retail business."

Rosie's manager was somewhat surprised at her quick response, and somewhat saddened by it. Now he was about to lose one of his most valuable employees. He quickly forgot about his loss and congratulated Rosie on her accepting the promotion. They went over a schedule for Rosie's move to the to the other store, and what paperwork she needed to complete for her promotion to be finalized. In all, it took about fifteen minutes for Rosie to complete everything and return to the sales floor.

That evening, Rosie carefully thought about the meeting that morning with her store manager, and the decision that she had made. She wondered, of course if it would the right decision as she sent the following coded message to her brother Tom:

The Eagle flies and lands on high,

As if to soar above the sky.

The trout has gone and swam upstream,

To be a better Eagle's team.

To see and saw and live anew,

Is the Union Square red, white and blue.

She felt that she was doing the right thing by accepting the promotion and staying with her employer, and that it would aid her in keeping her disguise intact. She wondered, though, how her brother Tom would see her decision. She would have to wait for his response and find out. Now for some microwave dinner and inexpensive wine. Wait! This is a celebration! This calls for the good stuff; this calls for Rosie to uncork the $7.95 bottle of "Lead Foot" Red Table Wine and have a glass in celebration. Regardless of what Tom's opinion is.

Red Table Wine and an episode of "To Tell The Truth" on TV. Life is good!

CHAPTER 20

Tom read the coded message from his sister Rosie with a smile on his face. He knew she would accept a promotion, if for no other reason than to keep her undercover looking legit. He also smiled at how little that company knew of value if they thought that she was ONLY store manager material, and nothing more. A Chief of Staff for a major medical center in New England, one of the top pediatric surgeons in the country; if they only knew. But, they didn't, and they won't. They promoted Rosie Johnson, not Helen Eldon, to a higher, probably something like an assistant store manager or possibly even a store manager, position and that was fine. Tom would send Rosie a coded message that he received her message, and go back to worrying about other things.

Things like the confirmations that were starting to come in on deliveries of his sixteen packages. Sixteen boxes of joy and excitement; not for the recipients, only for Tom.

Now Tom had to think about when he would call each recipient. Should he call immediately, or should he wait ten minutes, or maybe fifteen? He decided to call right away and get the program started. If he waited, he might miss someone; someone that he didn't want to miss connecting with.

Tom looked at the first confirmation, and slowly, very carefully dialed the cell phone number and listened. A male voice with a n accent answered the phone in Spanish. Tom just listened. Again the man on the other end of the call said something in Spanish, and at that precise moment, somewhere in Massachusetts a phone call went dead, an explosion went off, and a man went dead.

Confirmation number 2.

Confirmation number 3.

Confirmation number 4.

When Tom placed his phone call number 5 he was beginning to think that this was just way too easy. There could not be this many people that would open a box, a box without a return address, pick up a clock, pick up a cell phone, answer the phone when it started ringing with an old-time ringing telephone sound, and continue to hold the phone for ten more seconds. No, there just couldn't be, but there is!

The next five phone calls produced the same results and Tom kept thinking about the time when he was a small boy and his father had to dispose of a den of baby possums. He put some food outside the entrance to their den, and stood nearby with a rifle. As the babies came out of the den, Tom's father would put a single high-velocity, metal piercing, round through them and tell his little boy that "this is like shooting fish in a barrel." Tom understood his father's statement, but only now did he really appreciate its' meaning.

Tom had just completed his phone call number twelve when his home phone rang. He decided that the caller could wait, Tom has work to do; work of a very important nature. The caller was Tom's hardware store manager who left a message telling Tom that it was very important that he call him at the store. Tom told himself that it could wait and went about making phone call number thirteen. This time it almost sounded like a female voice had answered the phone, but Tom was not going to worry about gender; he had a message to send, and send it he is.

Tom's home phone rang again, and again Tom decided to avoid answering it. Again it was his manager asking Tom to contact him right away, there is an emergency and he needs to talk to Tom. Tom has more phone calls to make before he can return his manager's phone calls.

Tom could not believe how much good luck he was having with this project. Every single phone call was reaching its' intended person and Tom could, for the briefest fraction of a second, hear each bomb explode before the phone calls ended. If it wasn't that all this was killing off people, Tom might think it was fun. Not fun, but necessary. Necessary to Tom who had to avenge the murder of his brother George. "Revenge is mine, sayeth Tom" he kept telling himself. Mine, and no one else's.

Again Tom's home phone rang and this time his

manager sounded very stressed out when he left his message that the FBI was at the hardware store with a search warrant looking for something to do with some escaped murderer. Not finding Tom there, they gave the warrant to the manager, and the lead FBI agent dispatched some agents to go to Tom's home to try to find him. Tom's manager was calling to let Tom know that they are on their way.

"Crap!" Tom said to himself. "Just when I am having fun." Tom grabbed some papers and money from his desk drawers, retrieved an automatic pistol he kept in his closet, and tossed it all, along with his throw-away 'burner' phones, into a duffel bag and ran out the back door. He started to head for his BMW parked in the garage but discovered that he didn't have the right set of keys, so he jumped into his Jeep and drove rapidly out his driveway. He still had two more calls to make so he didn't want to drive very long.

Tom didn't realize that he missed running into the FBI agents by a mere four minutes as they drove into his driveway and surrounded his house. Tom only knew he was on the move and had tasks to finish.

Tom drove about ten minutes from his home into an area of town that was having grading done to it for the future building of homes. Tom couldn't drive long, and he didn't want to lose cell coverage by driving too far out of town. He left the engine running, just in case, and quickly looked over his list of confirmations.

Tom phone confirmation number fourteen. This time the phone rang and rang without an answer. Now Tom was getting nervous and wondered if, somehow, word had gotten around to the other members of the Mob. Finally a cranky, man with an accent answered the call and listened. He yelled into his phone just a micro-second before the explosion. Tom laughed to himself and said "teach him to yell at me!"

Tom had just finished dialing call number fifteen, when three all-black Suburbans drove past where he sat on a side street, and Tom knew who was inside each one. His most important phone call was next and it HAD to be made. Whether, or not, they saw him parked there, he had to place the phone call to Ernesto Siguenya. His phone call would be the best call of all.

As Tom looked for the confirmation of the delivery, he saw the last black Suburban start to slow down and head for an adjoining side street. Tom was getting nervous that he could not find a confirmation for delivery number sixteen. He knew that the boxes had all been delivered and that he should have gotten a confirmation for Ernesto's delivery, but there was not one. He anxiously went through every item he had and finally decided that he must have left it in his living room. It didn't matter to Tom as he saw the black Suburban make its' turn onto the side street and start in his direction. Seconds later, the other two Suburbans followed and were coming straight at Tom's location. Tom knew he had to place his phone call.

Tom carefully dialed the phone number. "Damn!" he said as he discovered he had misdialed the number. He quickly hung up and started to redial more slowly. One number by another number Tom dialed the phone number that he knew would make all this just so worthwhile. As Tom dialed the FBI agents were exiting their cars with guns drawn, as if they had just captured a wanted criminal. Shouting orders to Tom to "put everything down and put both arms out the window with your fingers spread apart", he continued dialing. This time he got the phone number right as he not only heard the ringing in the phone, but an echo, of sorts, ringing from his back seat in his Jeep.

Only two of the FBI agents were injured by flying metal fragments when the bomb, which was under a tarp in the back seat of Tom's Jeep, exploded and blew Tom, his Jeep and everything therein into mini-fragments of metal and body parts.

The agents' injuries did not appear to be serious, but they were driven to the hospital to be checked out anyway. They were quizzed by the doctors as to how they got metal fragments stuck in their arms and they told about the explosion that occurred. One attending doctor stopped his examination of one agent and asked if the agent had, in fact, said "Tom Kitchen"? When the agent confirmed his statement, the doctor told him that Tom Kitchen was an established, successful businessman within the community and wondered why he would have a bomb that exploded in his car. The agent sensed that he may have said too much already, told Dr. Chambers that he didn't know the answer to that question, only that it happened.

After finishing with the two FBI agents, Dr. Chambers went to find the phone numbers for the Ace Hardware store, the "About Time Clock & Jewelry" store, and the electronics supply store. Seems the Ace Hardware store is closed "for inventory", the clock & jewelry store is also closed "for inventory", and the electronics store is simply closed. He wondered what was going on in his little community, but finding out would have to wait. Right now, he has an interview with a reporter from CNN, who is waiting in his office upstairs.

Janice Wilkins was still hot on the trail of information regarding the Keeper House murders, and the people who may have been involved with them. Right now, though, she has a new blank in her search; a blank which needs to have facts filled in. A blank which is titled 'Tom Kitchen, Successful Small Businessman.' A blank she intends to find out more about, and fill in with those unknown facts.

But, for right now, Janice Wilkins of CNN has to interview Dr. Chambers of St. Vincent Medical Center. All other blanks will be filled in later...

It took weeks for the follow up investigation to confirm that Tom Kitchen was responsible for fifteen bombings which, themselves, were responsible for killing an estimated twenty seven members of the Mendoza Mob. From evidence found in Tom's home, there apparently was another bomb intended to be delivered to a distributor of jewels and jewelry named Ernesto Siguenya. That bomb was never picked up and delivered from Tom, but stayed in the back seat of Tom's Jeep without Tom being aware of it.

Tom Kitchen never knew what happened. It was over with within a micro-second.

Now, there really is only one "Keeper of the Key".

ABOUT THE AUTHOR

William Noel, a.k.a. Bill Noel, chooses to author his novels under the pen name of W.E. NOEL. Born in Philadelphia, PA, he was a child of movement and relocation. By the age of 8, when he settled in California with his grandparents, he had visited or lived in Canada and Mexico, and in 47 of the, then, 48 states. The oldest of 5 boys, and 1 girl, he spent his early years building careers in advertising, being a buyer for an international paper company, as a salesman, and finally, for his last 22 years of working, as president of a manufacturer's representative firm in Northern California. Bill resides, with his wife Kathleen, in the Bay Area and spends his retirement days traveling, golfing, and pounding the keys of his computer keyboard. He is currently researching storylines for several more novels; will any of them be about MURDER?

www.ingramcontent.com/pod-product-compliance
Lightning Source LLC
Chambersburg PA
CBHW062135170626
46813CB00002B/703